To Lee

signature
Lord LAMBOURN of ANDOVER

The
Conisbrough
Chronicles

GW00702671

The Conisbrough Chronicles

McMullen Country

Copyright © 2016 McMullen Country

The moral right of the author has been asserted.

Apart from any fair dealing for the purposes of research or private study,
or criticism or review, as permitted under the Copyright, Designs and Patents
Act 1988, this publication may only be reproduced, stored or transmitted, in
any form or by any means, with the prior permission in writing of the
publishers, or in the case of reprographic reproduction in accordance with
the terms of licences issued by the Copyright Licensing Agency. Enquiries
concerning reproduction outside those terms should be sent to the publishers.

This is a work of fiction. Names, characters, businesses, places, events
and incidents are either the products of the author's imagination
or used in a fictitious manner. Any resemblance to actual persons,
living or dead, or actual events is purely coincidental.

Matador
9 Priory Business Park,
Wistow Road, Kibworth Beauchamp,
Leicestershire. LE8 0RX
Tel: 0116 279 2299
Email: books@troubador.co.uk
Web: www.troubador.co.uk/matador
Twitter: @matadorbooks

ISBN 978 1785899 546

British Library Cataloguing in Publication Data.
A catalogue record for this book is available from the British Library.

Printed and bound in the UK by TJ International, Padstow, Cornwall
Typeset in 11pt Minion Pro by Troubador Publishing Ltd, Leicester, UK

Matador is an imprint of Troubador Publishing Ltd

MIX
Paper from
responsible sources
FSC
www.fsc.org
FSC® C013056

I am grateful to my children, Jessica Duncan and Eliot Lindsell for their advice, enthusiasm and talents in providing me with a finished article. I must also dedicate this work to my friends and acquaintances whose words, deeds and circumstances I have shamelessly reworked to create the Chronicles. It was nice knowing you.

Contents Page

Introduction

A thousand years ago in the Land of Con (close to the present day garden spot they call South Yorkshire) lived a wise, generous, kind but slightly ordinary looking man. His equally ordinary looking son, Padraig Con, was also blessed with the same traits and gifts as his father. But he also possessed a certain prescience – that rarest of qualities – that drove him to seek a bride and a partner of such immense charm and beauty so that generations to follow would inherit strength, wisdom and good looks. They were a shallow lot even in those days.

The Cons and their subjects lived in relative splendour and luxury. Many lived and worked in the imposing Castle Con on the hill overlooking the valley of the River Con that meandered through the land. Many family members and the local workers provided security for the area; many worked the land and the forests; the vast majority worked the mines which produced a rich and rare commodity. The Cons actively sought to expand wherever further mines could be sunk – an easy task in sparsely populated northern England. The homes in Con and wherever this dynasty spread its wings – even those of the lowest paid employees – were imposing and well constructed and families held these for life or for as long as they wished to remain employed by the dynasty. This was in sharp contrast to the Land of Sprot on the opposite bank of the river.

While Con was surrounded on three sides by dense, attractive woodland, was covered with all types of wild flower and was inhabited by birds and woodland creatures, Sprot had been stripped of anything useful by her rapacious inbred inhabitants. Few trees dared grow and anything that moved was skewered and gobbled down greedily by the lucky owner. Sprot dogs and cats had long since deserted this wasteland, running off with their tails between their legs (if they'd been lucky enough to retain them). Theft, drunkenness and violence reigned supreme in this lawless and soulless enclave – and the men weren't much better either. Living there was like being part of a Mad Max movie – only without the charity and integrity shown by those films' characters.

This "novella" or short story tells the true tale of the dynasty's journey through to the 21st century. The story is inspired, because we need all the help we can get, by the present day members of the dynasty who we count among our very best friends. Hopefully they won't sue us for damages but, hell, who cares? When this tale hits the Punch and Judy Book Club and the "Recently Reduced Bestsellers" list we won't care as we will be as rich as Croesus. We have been asked by thousands of libraries up and down the land how this story should be categorised. We think this is up to you, the reader, to decide but might we suggest either non-fiction or the "Total Drivel" section just above "Leisure Interests". Is the story suitable for children is another teaser that has been posed. Again this is up to you but, be warned; if your children don't read it they will grow up as chavs and probably develop hideous suppurating pustules on their buttocks.

Before we commence it might be worth giving you an insight and a bit of an introduction into some of the more noteworthy people and things you will meet on our journey through the ages. We think it might help because it sure is complicated:-

Lord Padraig Conisbrough – present day head of the dynasty with his wife

Lady Wendy Geek Geek – internet pioneer, contract bridge champion, self-proclaimed MILF and former Miss Billericay beauty queen 1958

Throughout the ages the Conisbroughs would uphold the tradition of calling the first born son Padraig – subsequent sons would be named Patrick, Palmerston and Paxman; daughters were named Patricia, Patsy, Peggy and Penny. Any children born of Patrick, Palmerston etc. would take whatever name the parents decided. By ascent Padraig or, often due to age, his son would be head of the dynasty. Through sound health, luck and good fortune the tradition has been unbroken these thousand years. The other extraordinary feature of the Conisbroughs has been their longevity with many family members living well into their nineties and beyond – in times when life expectancy was much lower than today. We are told this was due to a good diet and clean living. We think it was pure luck with the genetics and their shunning of even the tastiest and most alluring tobacco-based products

Sprots – the inhabitants of Sprot; anyone who doesn't read this book; or is not part of the dynasty. They are "normals"

usually identified by the pustules on their buttocks – or if you can't see their buttocks they can be distinguished by their scratching and itching motions

While many sprots come from – surprisingly – Sprot (now known as Sprotbrough) just across the river from Con they can be found anywhere these days and are usually up to no good

The Hotsprot Family – apart from the London train the only half decent product to emerge from Sprot. Henrietta (Henny) changed the family name to Hotbox in the Middle Ages. This Hotbox group has nothing to do with the musical Guys and Dolls – nothing!

Higson – squire to The First Lord Conisbrough. The Higson family have remained in service with the Conisbroughs to this day

Lord Somersby – buffoon, a purveyor of fruit drinks masquerading as something you might enjoy. Best known for his attempt to steal the concept of unreal histories from us

Cranbourne, Lanbourne, Ripoff and Scarper – advisors, accountants and lawyers to the dynasty throughout the ages

The Bully of Harlesden – briefly in charge of running London's railways (the dynasty's newest source of revenue) on behalf of His Lordship which is probably why we all go by bus. Massively overpaid and was constantly in dispute with Cranbourne, Lanbourne over petty cash receipts

Lord Lambourne of Andover – not to be confused with the nitpicking lawyers LLOA manages an estate in Hampshire; close ally of the dynasty

Baron Wilson (pronounced "Villsen") von Nettleham – runs a small independent fiefdom in Lincolnshire. Nettleham remains unconquered by the dynasty – probably because there is nothing there but a garage and a model railway shop

Sir Richard of Holton – sought an alliance with Nettleham when his treacle mine was subjugated by the dynasty and his black Labrador, Captain Charles Humber, forced in to slavery. Now the Baron's right hand man plotting revenge against the Conisbroughs

Treacle – the commodity at the heart of the dynasty's wealth and power. Treacle mines across the globe are all owned and operated by the Conisbrough dynasty or allied families

The Haverthwaites – a Lake District clan conquered by the Conisbroughs at the Battle of Lindall. Known for their laundry skills as evidenced by their ability to remove treacle from clothing. The battle (it was an arm wrestling contest in a local hostelry but battle sounds much more melodramatic and medieval) is remembered every year on 30th February at the "Celebration of the Subjugation"

Ayrton Speckmeister – short-sighted foreman of all Derbyshire treacle operations in the Middle Ages. Descendants of Ayrton would continue to work for the dynasty through the centuries

Graf Dieter von Dangelhosen – his Lordship's cousin in Cologne, Germany. Formerly in charge of the treacle operation in Europe but "retired" by the dynasty for his habit of hanging around railway stations exposing himself

Dynasty Timeline

1016 – 1035 Lord Con (details of his family unknown)

1035 – 1100 Lord Padraig Con (First Lord of Conisbrough) and wife Lady Gee Gee (aka Gigi) of Brough

1100 – 1168 Lord Padraig (Second Lord of Conisbrough)

1168 – 1240 Lord Padraig (Third Lord of Conisbrough) and wife Lady GoGo

1240 – 1301 Lord Padraig (Fourth Lord of Conisbrough)

1301 – 1381 Lord Padraig (Fifth Lord of Conisbrough)

1381 – 1449 Lord Padraig (Sixth Lord of Conisbrough)

1449 – 1520 Lord Padraig (Seventh Lord of Conisbrough)

1520 – 1585 Lord Padraig (Eighth Lord of Conisbrough) married Lady Grace Gu Gu, the Wolf Huntress

1585 – 1652 Lord Padraig (Ninth Lord of Conisbrough) married Lady Constance Ga Ga

1652 – 1748 Lord Padraig (Tenth Lord of Conisbrough) married Lady Gaw Gaw

1748 – 1815 Lord Padraig (Eleventh Lord of Conisbrough)

1815 – 1899 Lord Padraig (Twelfth Lord of Conisbrough) married to Lady Gertrude Gab Gab

1899 –1965 Lord Padraig (Thirteenth Lord of Conisbrough)

1965 – now Lord Padraig (Fourteenth Lord of Conisbrough) married to Lady Wendy Geek Geek

Part
One

Part One

The Celebration of the Communication

During his exploration of the wilds of East Yorkshire in search of opportunities to mine fresh treacle the young but not so handsome Padraig had come to know one Lady Gee Gee of Brough. This Brough is not to be confused with a place called Brough under Stainmore which is close by Clan Haverthwaite in Cumbria and occupied by sprots with the filthiest underwear in the kingdom.

Lady Gee Gee did not, as her name suggests, look like the rear end of a cart horse but was of extraordinary beauty and sturdy of leg and wrist. One would imagine her name should have been Gigi but the Broughs had yet to discover the letter "i". Padraig pleaded with his father to approach Earl Brough for her hand and this he agreed to do. Lady Gee Gee had, in turn, found Padraig's peculiar looks as fascinating as his wisdom and entertaining anecdotes. While on his travels Padraig would stay at Castle Brough never forgetting to bring Lady Gee Gee small gifts of unconscionably sweet treats that would have been enough to draw a sprot's teeth out. We think they're called Swirls these days. Padraig managed to convince Lady Gee Gee that it was the Scots (and not, as we all know, the Sprots) who invented the deep fried Mars bar.

How Lady Gee Gee giggled when Padraig regaled her with tales of sprots dropping like flies – blood supply to the brain having been cut off by the delicious calorific snack.

The union was not as smooth to arrange as Con and Brough had hoped; a rival for the affections of Lady Gee Gee was plotting to kidnap her from under the very noses of the pair. Dick Spraysprot of Sprot wanted to have Lady Gee Gee all to himself.

Now Sprot is just across the valley from Con separated only by the River Con. Neither group had anything to do with the other sharing no obvious talents or virtues in common. Indeed the sprots of Sprot were a wicked, conniving and sneaky crowd and remain so to this day should you come across one.

Dick Spraysprot planned to rally his fellow men of Sprot to intercept the wedding party on their way from Brough to Con, taking not only Lady Gee Gee but all the treacle and wedding gifts accompanying. Fortunately one of Padraig's employees, Ayrton Speckmeister, came to hear of this plot when Dick Spraysprot approached him for potential assistance in handling the stolen goods. Now Speckmeister was no fan of the Cons as he was a jealous and unsophisticated wildling from Chesterflood but he knew which side of his bread the treacle was on and informed Padraig Con of the plot. In exchange for this unfamiliar show of loyalty Padraig would reward him with a junior management position. Speckmeister's family work for the dynasty to this day but have sadly gained little in sophistication and breeding.

On her way to Con Castle Lady Gee Gee and her entourage would spend a full day on the road. There was no

M18 back in those days. Dick Spraysprot's evil and cunning plan was to intercept them at the end of their journey when the horses and the group itself were most tired and weak just before entering the Land of Con.

Now we've established that most sprots are stupid and Padraig was bright so it was no contest when Padraig suggested to them a "let's get to know one another" boating trip on the River Con with free treacle for every man taking part. That was all too much for the men of Sprot who clambered aboard the carefully prepared vessels for what would prove to be their final journey. Being greedy and oafish these men of Sprot refused to make room for women and children who remained on the river bank preferring to stuff themselves with sugary treats rather than give a care. This was to prove their undoing as Padraig, with help from his squire Higson, released all the vessels from their moorings and allowed them to slip away with their foolish cargo. Sprots can't swim so there was nothing for it but to let nature take her course.

Dick Spraysprot was left alone in the Land of Sprot with hundreds of women and children to fend for. Predictably, for sprots are no fans of hard work, he scuttled off westwards in the night leaving the women and children to fend for themselves. Dick made his way to Mold in Wales where he spent his days engaged in undue intimacy with a sheep called Sherbet. His ancestors still live in the area and, indeed, they run the local council when not out to pasture. As for the other men of Sprot, most were so bloated with treacle that they were clueless as to what was happening; others simply watched as they drifted east. When they finally came to a halt near the Con estuary they made no effort to return to

Sprot and settled where they had ended their journey. This was close to present day Goole – which explains a lot.

Many Sprot women made their way to Con and were integrated over the generations. Those that remained fared very well without the men folk and Sprotbrough exists to this day with its own boxing gym, branch of Wetherspoons, charity shop, treacle supermarket and social housing. Without the leadership of Dick Spraysprot, Sprot never posed any real threat to the Land of Con again.

The Celebration of the Conjugation

And so the conjoining of the Con and Brough families through the marriage of Padraig and Gigi created the first generation of the Conisbrough dynasty. The castle, abbey and the local branch of Greggs in Con were all renamed Conisbrough as part of the wedding celebrations and in honour of the couple. The wedding ceremony was a wondrous affair attended by the finest English and French nobility of the day and the service was conducted not by the abbot but by Cardinal Dewsnap of Saint Chrysanthemum on behalf of Pope Aspinall III himself. We understand royalty would have attended had they not all been busy bonking one another or bonking the Scots on the head with golf clubs.

Life in medieval times and in the Middle Ages was harsh and cruel but the dynasty did all it could to make life tolerable for its citizens and vassals. Lord Padraig established a new hospital for all subjects to use – though why Lady Gigi insisted there should be a herpes clinic included as part of the establishment remains a mystery to this day. The hospital and clinic were taken over by the NHS in 1985 and have made a loss ever since (apart from the WH Smith franchise which apparently makes a fortune).

Details of the Con (or Brough family for that matter) prior to the 11th century are sketchy but we must assume that the Cons had been in the valley for a number of generations. When interviewed for this story the present day Lord Conisbrough tried to insist that the family emigrated from the Eastern Roman Empire when it was overrun by the Caliphate – a sort of pre-Islamic State bunch of the Prophet's followers. This is impossible for a number of reasons according to our own research. First, you only need to watch the TV programme "Rome" to know those citizens in that part of the Roman Empire were staggeringly attractive, a trait missing from the Con dynasty until after the union of Padraig and Gigi. Second, we don't believe they would have been able to circumvent security and immigration controls at Calais and, lastly, there are a number of historical references to Con men being present in Sicily beyond the reign of Emperor Bogdan.

We are not historians but, thanks to Wikileaks, everyone knows that the Middle Ages marked a vast improvement in technology and agriculture and much of this is attributed to the Conisbroughs who invented the concept of feudalism while the rest of England was scratching their pustules or beating up the Scots and Welsh – laudable pursuits but they didn't really achieve anything. With their flourishing treacle mines a rich source of revenue for the Treasury the Conisbroughs were largely left alone, exempted from the ridiculous Crusades to Benidorm and Magaluf and other attempts to impose western values on innocent foreigners. The Conisbroughs set about establishing a dynasty based on commerce, a crime free society, free education, and health and welfare benefits for all citizens – and solid financial advice for those willing to pay their ridiculous eye-watering fees. With Lady Gigi behind him Lord Padraig was not only able to establish the first university at Willesden on the outskirts of London but he also formed the Conservative Party. If ever there was one thing for which we should all be thankful it is that.

The Celebration of the Consummation

But we promised you details of the marriage. Sadly no photographs of the occasion survive but some early brass rubbings and filigree etchings show Padraig and Gigi with their guests in a state of pure ecstasy after consuming a hog roast, four seasons pizzas and barrels of Kelham Island Pale Rider. We understand the event lasted for 48 hours without pause. It would have gone on longer for Lady Gigi was a woman of stamina and substantial appetites but, finally, Lord Padraig was carried away to his chambers by Higson. His laundry was sent to Haverthwaite for cleaning, repair and renovation but has yet to be returned.

An eager consummation followed the long and passionate seduction. At least on Gigi's part for Padraig was suffering from a severe state of flaccidity brought on by flagons of Pale Rider. It would have been like playing pool with a piece of rope. Initially it was nothing Lady Gigi couldn't cope with as she summoned Higson to bring duct tape and fresh cucumbers but as time went by and Padraig still showed no signs of stirring she started to look up train times back to Brough. But there was no need, for a couple such as this – clearly devoted to one another in that state of lovelyn where they felt connected at the soul on a mutual subconscious level where great co-dependency exists. Both felt that this love should be a sacred form of love that is ineffable. Unlike love or lust, lovelyn is much more sacred, and indulges the emotional and physical flaws along with the emotional and physical attributes as being beneficial to strengthening the tie and co-dependency of both parties involved. Lovelyn is also different from love because it requires that both parties feel the emotion in order for it to exist. Without the mutual co-dependency lovelyn cannot exist. A state of lovelyn must be entered subconsciously and cannot be changed by logic or reason. Religious terminology would allow us to explain this connection as a mutual connection of the soul. And then they finally got round to playing Mummy and Daddy.

The Maturation of the Melioration

Lady Gigi honoured the young Padraig with eight children – all healthy and handsome as they took after their mother for their looks and bearing while inheriting their father's intellectual acuity and love of Kinder eggs. In keeping with the Con custom the eldest son was christened Padraig – a tradition maintained to this day.

As we have hinted, and you know well from English history, these were dangerous, tyrannical and fearful times. Through its industry and self-sufficiency the dynasty remained protected from the poverty, subterfuge, bigotry and violence of the age – quietly going about its business and ensuring the Inland Revenue were paid in full. Threats to Conisbrough sovereignty in their territories were managed with diplomacy and, as necessary, resistance; the Conisbroughs always found a way out of difficult situations due to their vast resources and management capability. During the reign of King John they were indebted to a member of their staff called Lanbourne the Bald who was able to negotiate the dynasty out of the closest of close shaves by producing riches like a magician pulling a rabbit from his hat.

The passing of the baton from one Lord Padraig to his son was traditionally a happy affair without the mourning, wailing and gnashing of teeth normally associated with this everyday event. But one occasion one hundred years later had us wondering. On a courtesy visit to the Haverthwaites in Cumbria Lord Padraig and his eldest son Padraig were accommodated at the Anglers Arms, a particular favourite of his Lordship as his hosts would usually introduce a new beer to their guests. People don't realise the modern day phrase "Have a Thwaites" was introduced at Haverthwaite during that historic visit.

The Haverthwaites were not only launderers but brewers, citing the magical properties of the water from the adjacent River Leven. For Lord Padraig's visit they had brewed a special beer that went by the name of Thwaites Bitter. Great vats the height of the brewery building and solid oak casks of the ale were produced. During an inspection of one these vats Lord Padraig was leaning in to smell the hoppy aroma when he accidentally fell in. Efforts by the brewer, a hook nosed Germanic called Stefan Neumann, to save him were seemingly fought off by Lord Padraig who reports suggest prevented his own rescue.

These were austere and difficult times and Neumann was reluctant to dispose of the ale in order to recover Lord Padraig. So he summoned all the villagers and local gentry and slowly but surely reduced the beer level so that the late Conisbrough could be recovered. It was noted at the time that Lord Padraig had a smile on his face when taken out dripping and limp from the vat. A number of the villagers believed the mystery ingredient added colour, body (literally) and flavour to the Thwaites. Out of courtesy Neumann never brewed this ale again and the recipe was later sold to a sprot and Irish tinker called Chinless who lived near Lindall and whose family still market a stout under their name.

The new Lord Conisbrough was preparing to leave with his now dried out late father for the return journey when it is reported he saw his father's ghost. The ghost of his father said that he had been poisoned by the sprot Chinless which had made him giddy and fall. He invited his son to seek revenge on the sprot. Whether this is true or not we can't comment as it all sounds a bit theatrical. But it just so happened the cowardly Chinless had fled after the tragedy with his fellow sprots and had headed for Conisbrough and were to attempt to kidnap and ransom Padraig's better half, Lady Go Go as reprisal for the infamous humiliation of Dick Spraysprot some years earlier.

Fortunately it is a number of days ride between Haverthwaite and Conisbrough and sprots are not the best navigators we've ever encountered. Consequently the Conisbrough party not only arrived back home ahead of the Chinless group but the celebrations of the new Lord Padraig Conisbrough's inauguration had been completed. Stefan Neumann had kindly provided several (small) barrels of foaming ale complete with warning panels for the event. Later the Conisbroughs would recruit Neumann to take charge of their national brewing operation.

Lord Conisbrough's squire, Higson, was returning barrels to Haverthwaite some days later when he and his escort, Lady Patricia Conisbrough, eldest daughter of the late Lord, encountered the Chinless group. While Higson was slight of frame and of advancing years Lady P was an imposing young woman and growing up with four brothers was more than combat ready. This was not to prove necessary as the Chinless wonders didn't recognise Higson or Patricia and merely asked directions to Conisbrough. Lady Patricia promptly pointed the grateful party in the direction of Mold where they might meet up with the Spraysprots. It is said they arrived six months later.

The Disaffection with the Infection

As we know the population of Sprot was severely depleted during what shall be named "The River Con Treacle Massacre" but sprots from other parts of the kingdom slowly descended on the mainly female inhabitants and, by the early 14th century, numbers had stabilised. Sadly for the people of Sprot matters were about to take another turn for the worse.

Our history books tell us that the Black Death probably had its origins in China and spread via rats and fleas into Europe. We know this to be nonsense as the source of the plague – which impacted on most of Europe wiping out millions – was Sprot. A food vendor by the name of Henny (Henrietta) Hotsprot allowed a pair of her undergarments to fall from her wash line into a large bowl of treacle salad she had been preparing for sale to her fellow sprots. We strongly suspect that those undergarments had not been laundered to the high standard we're accustomed to witnessing from the Haverthwaites and were riddled with the discharge from suppurating pustules. The Black Death was born. With this any semblance of social order that existed in Sprot decayed with the corpses. It was almost as if the laws of nature were seeking to redress some kind of balance.

Henny Hotsprot's salads were extremely popular and so the crunchy green agony spread quickly and virulently throughout Sprot and beyond. Remarkably Henny and her children survived – probably due to a perverse form of immunity caused by eating her own preparations and building up resistance to the killer bacteria. Her fellow sprots never once suspected that she and her green goodies were the source of their illness (despite sprots usually being wary of fresh vegetables). Rather fortuitously Henny could see the writing (and where people had been sick) on the wall and crept unseen out of Sprot with her children.

Sprot became more of a wasteland than hitherto and, because of the lack of hygiene, poor diet and filth everywhere you looked, it was regarded as a no-go area and so the usual traders wisely steered a wide berth leaving the good folk of Sprot to their own devices. Apart from throwing bodies in the river there was no activity in the town whatsoever. Imagine a scene from "The Walking Dead" without the survivors and you would be getting close.

Retire from the Fire

Henny was a good woman at heart despite being trodden on all her young life. The sprot male in whose hut she had been living, Tom Butchersprot, had deserted her some years before when she was expecting their second child in the space of a year. Dumb Tom, as he was known, didn't say a lot and what he did say wasn't worth hearing. One day, according to his sister, he had just upped and left – heading to Goole in search of better paid work, apparently – without saying a word to Henny or the baby. The sister, Angelina Potsprot, in typical sprot fashion and displaying all the positive attributes associated with Sprot, now wanted the hut. As Henrietta and Dumb Tom had not married (few sprots did after an incident some years earlier when a brother and sister were married by mistake by a drunken friar) Angelina would have more claim if push came to shove.

Indeed the pushing and shoving had already started in the shape of the brute of a man Angelina lived with. Neal Spudsprot thought he owned the place – probably because he had a few of the brain cells in existence in the area. Spud paraded around Sprot wearing a silk kimono-style garment which he had stolen from a trader in the market at Goole and thought he looked impressive. He certainly made an impression but it wasn't really a positive one. We think he was probably suffering from an "Emperor's New Clothes" situation as nobody dared to tell him what a plonker he looked merely said good morning and sniggered. Spud had threatened to burn down Henny's hut many times but, possessing more of those valuable brain cells than her adversary, Henny realised that, while still possible in all the circumstances, if the hut was what they wanted Angelina was unlikely to sanction its destruction. Any harm coming to Henny or the children would have the guards crawling all over them and doubtless a trip to York for justice.

Nevertheless Henny set about defending the hut should Angelina or Neal try anything. Her name Hotsprot had come from her mother and she despised it. This woman had taught Henny very little but she had explained that nothing stopped intruders, robbers or bullies quicker than a pan of hot water – hence she was given the "title" Hotsprot for being a dab hand with her kettle. Henny set up a similar defence with a pot of water on the fire in readiness but it proved unnecessary. She was a touch relieved that it only proved precautionary as the last thing she wanted was to emulate or behave as her mother had.

Long before everyone began falling ill and when it was clear Dumb Tom wasn't coming back anytime soon Henny had been thinking seriously of trying to find somewhere better for her children, preferably in the opposite direction to that taken by their father. The sale of the food she grew and prepared kept the three of them from starving but only just. Having made up her mind and explaining the plan to the children she collected what meagre belongings and money they could carry and took the children to the edge of the sprawling town and instructed them to wait a few minutes for her return. Henny had one fond farewell to make and she did so by burning her hut to the ground.

Rounding on one of their own like a pack of voracious dogs the objective men of Sprot were baying for yet more blood urged on by the women. Like a group of plump senoras fluttering their fans at the corrida, the female segment of Sprot had some sympathy for Henrietta fearing the same could happen to them at the hands of the awful Spudsprot. Only the presence of the Conisbrough militia – not intervening but watching carefully from the edge of Sprot, having been drawn by the flames – prevented Spud from being peeled, pricked and thrown on his own fire.

In the weeks following everyone in Sprot continued to point the finger at Neal Spudsprot saying he had murdered Henny and her babies as, to be fair, he had made more than enough loud, boastful threats that the whole of Yorkshire must have known his intention. The Sheriff finally authorised the petrified Spudsprot's arrest (it had been difficult finding anyone willing to venture into the diseased and ravaged Sprot to grab him) and after two weeks in chains in the prison at Wakefield Neal Spudsprot was brought before the magistrate, still wearing his kimono but slightly more soiled and split, accused of three murders. Fortunately for Spud investigators could find no human bones or other significant remains in the fire and a witness came forward to say the Hotsprot family had fallen victim to the plague – and the fire was a terrible accident and a coincidence.

The witness, Harry Kumquatsprot, who had a soft spot for the clot Spudsprot was duly primed and rewarded by

Angelina Potsprot, and had earned a year's wages and Spud's kimono in half an hour to save his friend from further incarceration or much worse. Harry was another of those products of the Sprot inter-breeding programme with a huge quiff and some of the dodgiest crooked teeth you've ever seen to go with his cheesy optimism and eye for a scam. Some months later Harry, swiftly drinking his bribe money away on a kind of medieval pub crawl binge that took him to every tavern between Sheffield and Chesterflood, saw Henny large as life but, desperately trying to think of ways of fiddling more money from the situation, he realised that he would be brought before the magistrate for lying if he were to reveal her whereabouts now.

Harry let the matter rest and had another drink instead. For a brief moment he'd considered blackmailing Henny but could see no way out of it for himself without a pan of hot water down his trousers or a fire in his hut. Harry retired to his temporary lodgings at a local tavern where he intended sleeping on the dilemma. Unfortunately Harry was arrested before he could formulate any sort of money-making plan and charged with indecency for dancing with his kimono untied at the window of his room without having first drawn the chintz curtains.

Well Shot of Sprot

Walking for a whole day Henny found herself in a place called Chesterflood. After a few hiccups (literally, as the gin was of poor quality) she and the children settled there and were to set up what soon became a thriving small business. Over the generations branches of the popular food outlet she would introduce would open across the nation. Henny's original shop front survived until recently taken over by Wetherspoons. Ingeniously she changed her name so as not to be recognised as the Lady of Death from Sprot and rather than just selling salad began selling warm bread and meat in small square polyethylene boxes. The miners, tradesmen, guards and womenfolk all called her Little Miss Hotbox.

Back in Sprot all kinds of ridiculous rumours about the cause of the fatal sickness were doing the rounds but Henny was not mentioned as it was the semi-official outcome that she had perished from disease and been thrown in the River Con with all the other victims. First, the Cons had somehow infected their food with a tainted batch of treacle; second, Dick Spraysprot had returned and was exacting revenge on whoever he could find; and, lastly, that Sprot had somehow upset the Turnip Gods they worshipped and the Great Lord Bulbous Taproot was showing his displeasure. Nobody got close to the truth and, consequently Henny Hotsprot, soon to become Hotbox, was off the hook. Her family would continue to enjoy good fortune for generations to come. The same could not be said for the vomiting inhabitants of Sprot many of whom would perish and end up on a hook awaiting their turn for disposal.

Those sprots able bodied enough attempted to build rudimentary catapults to fling infected corpses across the Con into Conisbrough but the weight proved too much. What material did manage the journey was eagerly consumed by the wild pigs of Conisbrough to no ill effect. Indeed Conisbrough escaped the worst of the disease altogether thanks to the physical separation from Sprot that is the River Con and the most sophisticated medical care available. Historical records indicate one member of the Conisbrough dynasty perished during the years the disease was rampant. Reports on the exact cause and circumstances differ as it was rumoured Peggy Conisbrough was playing golf naked in a lightning storm at the time having consumed too much of Stefan Neumann's fine ale at a christening ceremony.

The Refinement of the Refreshment

We're not sure whether it was in reaction to Lord Conisbrough's untimely passing or simply a love of the product but the dynasty in the form of the newly inaugurated Lord Padraig and his uncle Palmerston invited Stefan Neumann to take a sabbatical from Haverthwaite and see what he could do with the water from the free flowing River Con and hops and barley brought to nearby brew houses from a place far to the east called Lincolnshire. Padraig and Palmerston hoped the fruit of Neumann's labours would soon be equally free flowing in the taverns of Conisbrough.

Neumann, as the shrewd and discerning amongst you might have gathered, was not a native of Haverthwaite. Such was the standard of beer and brewing in his native Germany that Neumann was considered a veteran in the field of mediocrity and, with his assistant brewers, Koln Minns and Johann Bibliothekar, had been chased out of his hometown of Cologne for failing to apply the strict rules in place to his brewing techniques. Neumann, while a true nourisher of inebriants, was also accused of adding his own fluids to the recipe on occasions.

A tall and imposing man when sober Neumann found

it impossible to secure employment in Germany with his reputation and so headed for France. As we all know, the French know nothing about beer and, worse still, are unwilling to learn. Neumann considered Belgium as a location for a fresh start but the monks had the industry closed off cartel-style. The tonsured tipplers made Neumann very uncomfortable with their lack of appreciation for his talents and, to be fair to Neumann, he would never have come to terms with their style of brewing and the overuse of treacly compounds.

After six months on the road, drifting from tavern to tavern, making a living by brewing the occasional barrel for appreciative landlords in England, the Neumann group ended up at Haverthwaite. All they had heard about the water purity in the north of England was true and they soon had a solid reputation and a substantial customer base. With the Conisbrough logistics and distribution network at his disposal Neumann beers were enjoyed from Cumbria to Con. Probably wishing to avoid another incident and avoid the risks on the journey between Haverthwaite and Conisbrough Palmerston brought Neumann and his men to the Brewery Tap.

Nobody was aware of it at the time but Neumann had become weary of Haverthwaite. While the brewing conditions and water were perfect for his trade he and his assistant brewers had grown tired of the climate with the cold and driving rain of Cumbria. Added to that the stigma that still lingered following the accident with the late Lord Conisbrough and the rolling stone that was Neumann was ready for a change of scenery.

Neumann's reputation as a potential troublemaker was no secret to the Conisbroughs due to their connections with the Dangelhosens in Cologne, a family with which they did business and maintained close connections, but they believed it worth the risk. Shortly after his arrival they could be forgiven for wondering if they had made the right call. One night after a few orange juices in the Brewery Tap Neumann detected sprots stealing treacle from his store room and sent word with one of his assistants to the Red Lion where the on duty militia were posted. His assistant returned some minutes later to say that the militia could spare nobody to attend but would follow the matter up in the morning. Neumann told his assistant to return to the Red Lion and advise the guards that he had cut the throats of three sprots and three others had fled into the castle grounds. Almost instantly a platoon of archers, armoured carts and a dozen pike men had arrived at the Brewery Tap to find two sprots filling bags with treacle. "I thought you said you'd cut their throats?" asked the Chief Guard. "I thought you said you had nobody available" retorted Neumann.

Time Gentlemen Please

Nearing the end of his six month sabbatical Stefan Neumann was pleased with the results having produced some lively and exquisite beers for the dynasty members and the local taverns. Time had not permitted a more mass produced product and so the ales were mainly for local consumption. This had the effect of drawing customers from far and wide to sample the Neumann offerings, in much the same way as Haverthwaite was a Mecca for the connoisseurs. Traders bringing goods for sale in Conisbrough market would now routinely spend a night or two in the comfortable rooms above the tavern after a meal and a bellyful of ale deferring the journey back to the tedium of their home lives.

When Euan Lanbourne, Lord Conisbrough's bookkeeper and descendant of Lanbourne the Bald, undertook his half yearly audit of the tavern's accounts he could scarcely believe what he was seeing on the ledger in front of him. Profits from the sleepy Conisbrough tavern had quadrupled. While the landlady, Juanita Busenfeld, had taken quite a shine to the free-spirit that was Neumann, her eyes opened even wider with delight on receiving the news that the tavern had been so successful. She begged Lanbourne to force Neumann to stay. If there was one person who could persuade Neumann to stay on longer it was not the disagreeable, crusty and ill-tempered Lanbourne.

Like Neumann, Juanita was an émigré from Germany and had arrived in Conisbrough as a child with her father and Spanish mother who were given positions under Higson up at the castle, having previously worked with the Dangelhosens in Cologne. From the castle kitchen she had graduated to assisting in the Red Lion in the village and then to managing the much larger Brewery Tap. She had eight staff under her, excluding the brewers who reported to Euan Lanbourne, comprising two stable boys who cleaned and ran errands as necessary, a cook and her assistant and four girls who had recently left school, who would wash, clean and serve as necessary.

Juanita had a substantial skill set but most impressive of all was her memory and attention to detail. While she had little to do with Koln Minns and Johann Bibliothekar they would frequently enter the tavern with fresh barrels, set them up ready for pouring and remove empties. A small bearded man, Johann would shuffle about barely lifting his feet off the floor. Juanita referred to him as Zwerg or Gorgojo depending on which language she was speaking at the time – neither of which sound particularly polite.

Although not a wealthy man by any measure, Johann possessed a varied and colourful collection of neckerchiefs kept in a linen bag on a hook in the stable – one for each day of the month. If ever Johann wore the same neckerchief in the same month Juanita and her staff would tease and taunt until he shuffled off bemused back to his brewery. But Juanita's main party trick was to address the baffled brewer in front of all her customers by saying "Not tonight, Johann, I have a headache" at which she, along with all her customers, would scream with laughter.

For his part the new Lord Padraig, despite being aware of all the obvious advantages, would not be coaxed in to approaching Neumann on the subject of his staying on. His view was that he had entered in to an agreement with his friends and business associates in Haverthwaite and he would have no part in untangling that arrangement. Neumann and his assistants were oblivious to all the drama in the background and cared little for Lanbourne's balance sheet – and even less for Lanbourne himself.

It wasn't the luxurious accommodation that would have swayed the three brewers in to staying because they had spent the previous five months residing in the stables by the tavern. While Juanita Busenfeld had, of course, encouraged them to use the facilities in the tavern and to take a hot bath when they wished only Neumann had taken up her offer.

It was on one of these occasions that Juanita, sending the serving girls away on some trifling errand, took it upon herself to assist Neumann with his ablutions. So successful did her efforts with her 14-inch loofah prove that Neumann was unable to walk the next day and promptly decided to remain in Conisbrough if he was welcome. Lord Padraig arranged it so that the Haverthwaites, who had a brewing operation far larger than theirs, would have Neumann at their disposal in the summer months each year. In fact the Haverthwaites never asked for him to return.

Juanita was a striking looking woman with the black hair, olive complexion and outgoing nature of her mother and the height, strength and business acumen of her father who had been Dangelhosen's cellar man and an assistant brewer all his life. The previously untameable Neumann was utterly and completely trapped – and loved every second of it.

Juanita and Neumann decided to marry and Her Ladyship suggested that they might like to have their ceremony at Conisbrough Abbey – and they had a traditional German service courtesy of the knowledgeable abbot almost immediately. This honour normally only fell to the Conisbrough family and demonstrated the high esteem in which Neumann and Busenfeld were held. This gesture also said much for the Conisbrough's inclusive relationship with their employees. On the day of the ceremony Neumann was again barely able to walk but, such were the attractions of the multi-talented Juanita that he was able to make it thanks to a lift up the hill in one of Johann Bibliothekar's carts. For their part, Bibliothekar and Minns remained in Conisbrough too but, for reasons that escape us, preferred to stay in the stable with the assortment of animals that joined them on a regular basis.

In the Land of the Blind the Man with the White Stick is King

By strange coincidence Ayrton Speckmeister was making his way along the same road that Henny Hotbox and her children had taken just twenty four hours ahead of him as he returned to his home in Chesterflood from Conisbrough. Speckmeister was junior manager of the treacle mining operations in Derbyshire answering to Paxman Conisbrough. The disappearance of several sacks of treacle from the mine in Bolsover was a serious matter and he had been summoned to Yorkshire to explain himself to both Paxman and His Lordship.

It was raining on the Yorkshire Derbyshire borders as he squelched his way up hill and down dale and through dense forest and woodland. Speckmeister's great great grandfather had been promoted to the mining operations job years earlier and Speckmeister and his father before him did their best to hold the job down given their lack of any common sense and, significantly, their poor eyesight which passed down through the generations and often caused amusement to those around him and a deep sense of shame and sadness to Speckmeister himself. As a child at Chesterflood Primary School he had been teased mercilessly by the other pupils (mainly sprots) for his feeble performances at football, rugby and, in particular, cricket. The trouble was he just couldn't see the ball.

Carrying this myopia into adulthood Speckmeister had by and large learned to manage the situations in which he found himself. Once he took a wrong turn en route home to Chesterflood from Conisbrough after another bollocking at the hands of His Lordship and very nearly ended up in Mold with the Spraysprots. It was only the unholy stench and strange affectionate behaviour of the sheep that alerted him to his error. Fortunately Speckmeister had retained the ability to run he had perfected in the playground years earlier. On another occasion he had held a formal meeting with his superintendents at Oxcroft treacle mine only to find out later that his staff had placed dummies filled with straw at the seats around the meeting room table and had all disappeared to a local beer festival instead.

One person who didn't laugh at his predicament was Henny Hotbox when they were to meet some weeks later. As a sprot and a single mother Henny had done her fair share of fighting for her livelihood and had no time for mocking others' misfortunes.

Cranbourne Again Christian

Euan Lanbourne, Lord Padraig's bookkeeper, was a member of a family that had lived in Conisbrough longer than anyone could remember. There are no records of when the first Lanbourne (or Cranbourne, for that matter) came to the Con Valley but there is mention of both family names in the Abbey records pre-dating Padraig Con's arrival in the area. We presume this first mention is an indication that the "original" Cranbourne and Lanbourne were monks. That may be so but it doesn't answer how they had children and the line continued. We don't know much about abbeys and monks so we'll let them off. Apparently some were better behaved monks than others. What we do know is that Cranbourne and Lanbourne were accomplished in reading, writing and arithmetic through their studies at Con Abbey – attributes passed on to future generations. It's just rather a shame those were the only positive benefits later Cranbourne, and in particular Lanbourne, creations would inherit.

We might be reading more in to the effect of an ecclesiastical upbringing but our view is that it did as much harm as it did good. You never know how much perversion and exploitation there was in the environment. Actually it's not hard to imagine that there was plenty of potential. In one respect it was healthy that successive Lord Conisbroughs shunned the bigotry and fervour at the abbey; the second Lord of Conisbrough once said that he would gladly attend regular worship at the abbey when warfare, political wrangling, poverty, disease and greed had been eradicated from the kingdom – until then he had neither the time nor the desire to listen to the abbot pontificate. Others were welcome to attend and would doubtless tell him all about it.

Cranbourne's diaries tell us that the abbot, catching the young Euan fiddling about under his bed covers for the umpteenth time, asked the boy if he was addicted to masturbation and that he should reach out to him so they might beat it together. Put your hand in faith and not down your breeches, was the favourite catchphrase of the abbot – though it clearly didn't apply when it was his hand down the breeches. Modern day experts in this field suggest that the scarring from such a hands on education is deep, permanent and negative behaviours are easily passed on to following generations. Just as an aside we weren't sure how you became an expert on the subject of molestation. "Sorry, you don't have the necessary experience" or "The examples you've provided lack penetration" etc.

In any event the damaged goods that was Euan Lanbourne was one of the wealthiest men in the valley and, with his friend and business partner, Augustus Cranbourne, they had carved a niche for themselves not only as bookkeepers to every business within miles but advisors to His Lordship on all matters fiscal. There was nothing the two of them didn't know about tax – which came in handy when the monarchy ran a bit short and sent a few platoons to collect. They were both part-time teachers at the abbey as well, in the local place of learning Padraig had established for the children of Conisbrough and, occasionally, at the university at Willesden. By all accounts they were very good teachers – never distracted and firmly enamoured with their specialist subjects of accountancy and financial irregularity. Well paid for all of these discrete activities Cranbourne Lanbourne took rooms and later purchased land in what is present day Stratford in London. Whatever it was they got up to in the south was clearly profitable – and probably immoral. They had all the qualities to flourish in the company of the whey-faced poltroons and other assorted wretched incumbents of the royal court at that time.

How Do You Do,
Ripoff and Scarper

Nobody was prepared to talk to us about how the present day firm came to be known as Cranbourne Lanbourne Ripoff and Scarper but we believe we've tracked down the individuals concerned that added that certain style, sophistication and *je ne sais quoi* to the firm's title. Although these four individuals didn't form a company until much later they were business associates from the very early days of the dynasty and more than likely introduced His Lordship to the opportunities to trade with the Dangelhosens in Cologne.

A regular at the Brewery Tap where he insisted on having his own reserved table Lanbourne was especially fond of a tipple. Juanita, the Landlady, had little choice but to grant Euan his wish as he provided a good service as bookkeeper and seemed favoured by the dynasty. His large table was against a wall in the far corner of the tavern where Lanbourne could set out his papers and observe everyone and everything that happened. Juanita advised Neumann on more than one occasion that she was discomforted by Lanbourne's crafty, beady eyes following her around the tavern as she went about her business serving food and drink and supervising her staff. Neumann could understand, not that Juanita merited supervision, because the larger than life landlady rarely paused for breath, singing, smiling and chattering away to anyone who would listen. Neumann could hardly take his eyes off his beautiful wife and easily understood why the oily Lanbourne would feel similarly afflicted.

One other feature noted by Juanita and Neumann was that no matter who sat at his table with him Lanbourne never once ordered a drink for his guest but rapaciously accepted whenever one was offered. There were plenty of wannabes eager to get in to Lanbourne's good books and two raddled and seedy individuals who were regular visitors from the south were Roger Ripoff and Scarper Knightly, a lawyer and an official at the Royal Court respectively. The one thing observers noticed that all these men had in common was their inability to smile. Presumably they were too busy making money or developing schemes to do so and reserved their smiling for more private moments having relieved someone of their stash of cash.

They weren't too busy to drink vast quantities of wine and ale though and consequently weren't clever enough to keep a number of their money making schemes private from the astute Juanita and, by association, Neumann. Stefan the Brewer had been eager to get his own back on Lanbourne after losing money to him in the tavern. Never having been beaten before with his three cups and one coin trick Lanbourne proceeded to win seventeen times in a row much to Neumann's disgust, Euan's delight and Juanita's amusement.

Neumann's revenge was sweet and left egg on the faces of the Cranbourne Lanbourne mafia. To our knowledge this was the first and last time this happened. Juanita had heard Lanbourne discussing the group's decision to make a sale of treacle to Sprot in exchange for a quantity of ore that the sprots had likely stolen. Ore was useful in the manufacture of armour, shields and weapons that the militia and Conisbrough guards used so Neumann, who had his own supplies of treacle in his storeroom as an ingredient for dark beer or porter, undercut the price Euan had asked for the treacle and took the ore back to the brewery. When the men hired by Lanbourne came back from Sprot empty handed with the treacle consignment intact the blood vessels on Euan's forehead started throbbing as the selfless entrepreneur had already promised the consignment of ore to the local smithy and had greedily accepted a significant advance.

Discussing his dilemma at his usual table in the Brewery Tap with Cranbourne that evening Euan was at first surprised to hear that Juanita knew of a supply of ore she would be able to persuade the owner to sell if Lanbourne needed it. A look of delight was followed by realisation slowly drifting across Lanbourne's puffy features but, of course, there was nothing he could do about it – mainly as his reputation within the area was at stake. Euan sensed that any transaction involving Juanita would be insufficiently private and asked for her complete discretion. "That will cost you extra, my dear Euan" she whispered, getting deliberately and indecently close to one of his reddening piggy ears. Euan wasn't sure the little shiver that ran through his corpulent frame was caused by the proximity of the fragrant Juanita or the crippling financial loss he was about to experience. We suspect the latter.

The Distraction of
the Infraction

The Conisbroughs – rightly or wrongly depends on your view – took advantage of the devastation that was the Black Death by spreading dynasty wings across the nation. To the south most males over the age of 14 had either perished or been conscripted for service in the war against France which seemed to go on forever. Conisbrough expansion met with little resistance from the womenfolk tending the land. In fact they welcomed the intrusion, the economic benefits a local mine or construction venture would bring. The inns and shopkeepers flourished and, significantly, the fair minded and benign style of the Conisbroughs by and large did not upset local landowners or the equilibrium of local life.

While this was true of the north and east (these days an area stretching from Huddersfield to Goole in the east, York in the north and Northampton in the south) the same could not be said of London and the rest of the south of England. Slowly and inexorably discontent grew culminating late in the 14th century with the Pedants' Revolt. People had become so burdened down and tired of taxation, war, taxation and more war that a debating society was formed by some influential landowners and despatched to all parts of the country to influence opinion and improve the appalling grammar of royal proclamations. (ed. Should that be a capital letter on royal?).

The group's debates were well attended by the townsfolk wherever they established a meeting. Such was the puffed up self-importance and arrogance of some of the participants that many in the audience thought the event a sophisticated form of free theatre. The pompous airbags would go on for ages debating the merits and demerits of the split infinitive until one of the audience would interrupt asking about the future of taxation and social housing availability. This would send the panel, radiant in self-love, into paroxysms of spluttering and coughing as these were subjects, of course, about which they knew nothing.

To take revenge on the locals the group would overturn the carts and stalls with any item of produce misspelt or with an apostrophe in the wrong place. We dare say you've noticed that support for those plucky shopkeepers who stood up against the pedants persists to this day with market stall holders proudly offering their finest apple's for sale at two pound's a kilo.

Euphoria in Myopia

Henny Hotbox as she was now calling herself had, you will recall, arrived in Chesterflood with her children but little else. While her departure from Sprot had been voluntary in truth she had little by way of belongings and money to form the basis of a fresh start. She did have her wits, a keen eye for an opportunity and a background in catering.

The situation in Chesterflood while a hundred times better than in Sprot, due to the medical facilities made available, was still dire if you had no work, no money and nowhere to live. Henny had obtained a room for herself and her family at a tavern and had largely paid her way by cleaning, serving the customers and helping in the busy kitchen. Her talents with an iceberg lettuce were as obvious as her love of gin and on many fronts the landlord was happy to have her stay.

After a few weeks Henny rented a stall in the market selling her own brand of treacle salad and the bread and meat she was able to cook in the tavern's kitchen with the landlord's blessing. On her first day the short sighted Ayrton Speckmeister was one of her first customers. Pointing, as he thought, at one of the treacle salads on offer, Henny served him the beef in a bread roll. Historical records of what happened next are thin and sketchy but we believe

Speckmeister uttered the words "Bugger me" as the delicious cut of beef and the juices melted in his mouth with the soft lightly baked bread that was Henny's trademark.

Henny obviously misheard her customer because she thought he said "Burger" and, not knowing the words and ways of the people of Chesterflood, believed her beefy creation to be a burger. In that one moment history was changed and Henny had set up the first burger stall. Sadly her creation would be passed on to others to promote as she would soon move out of the catering business and on to bigger and better things.

Speckmeister was a shy and timid young man who lived with his mother and sister. His mother, Josephine, was known for miles for the size of her doughnuts and so Speckmeister was no stranger to high quality food. Over the coming days he would return to Henny's stall and, although pointing in the direction of the burgers, was occasionally served with a salad. No matter as Speckmeister was mesmerised by Henny Hotbox. Standing by her stall eating his lunch he would listen to the other customers, to the banter that Henny seemed happy to trade with the miners and farm workers who came in search of her wares.

A few days later Speckmeister found Henny in what could best be described as a state of anxiety and bewilderment surrounded by some local officials from the council who he had seen some time ago inspecting his mother's doughnuts. It seemed Henny had to register her stall and complete formalities that would make Henny liable for national and local taxes while qualifying for the many entitlements that being employed in Chesterflood brought with it.

Summoning up immense courage Speckmeister intervened – though at his first attempt he went to the wrong stall and began a conversation with a fishmonger – but recognising the young employee of the Conisbrough dynasty the officials' mood softened and they explained the requirement and the necessary paperwork Henny had to complete.

Henny asked young Speckmeister if he could help and agreeing to do so turned up at the tavern that evening to assist with the formal registration of Henny's business and completion of a tax declaration. Henny Hotbox seemed bemused at the prospect of handing over a chunk of her profits to strangers but slowly and carefully Speckmeister explained that, in return, should she fall on hard times, she would be protected; she would be entitled to a small house in exchange for rent; her children would receive education and a meal at lunchtime while she was working; and in the event of illness or worse still the plague medical attention was freely available.

The slightly less bemused, relaxed (she'd had a couple of gin and tonics) Hotbox had heard stories of such places when back in Sprot but the legendary Dick Spraysprot and other senior figures had always said that only the hoity toity Conisbroughs across the River Con enjoyed such privileges. That evening with the shy Speckmeister explaining things to her gently and sensibly Henny smiled for the first time in many a year (she'd had a couple more gin and tonics by then and the landlord would be sorry to see her move out).

With her affairs in order the hard working Henny put the filthy and insidious world of Sprot far behind her. As we will gather through the generations not all sprots were as gross and bile inducing as Dick Spraysprot. Many were for sure, being lazy worthless cretins with a vacancy where the brain should live but Henny and, so it would prove, her children and their families down the ages were not.

Many of you must be asking why and how a sprot can waltz in to Chesterflood and settle so easily. The answer, of course, is that very few did for the reasons expressed above. It was not about being a sprot, a Conisbrough, a Germanic brewer or a Haverthwaite laundryman – there were no Chesterflood border control officials – it was about being a worthwhile contributor to society. Such a philosophy and ideology began in Con with Lord Padraig and extended across areas where the dynasty had influence. Such wondrous principles of fairness and justice would be taken forward by the Conservative Party for the benefit of future generations.

Paxman Turns
On Overdrive

Chesterflood, in common with many small market towns where the dynasty operated, grew in size of population keeping house builders and stall holders like Henny busy. The mining operations thrived with a good source of local labour and an efficiently managed supply chain for the treacle sucked from the mines. By the Middle Ages Chesterflood was three times the size of Conisbrough. His Lordship had no desire to metamorphose Conisbrough in to an urban metropolis preferring to retain its unique tranquillity, beauty and harmony.

In truth large numbers of people born in Conisbrough, including the children and grandchildren of His Lordship, would move on, finding work and a home elsewhere, often running a district mining operation, distributing the locally produced treacle and ale far from Conisbrough wherever new markets for the product could be uncovered.

So Conisbrough remained the sleepy small town that it is today. Aside from the castle which was a truly magnificent edifice, towering over the valley and the surrounds watching carefully like a bitch guarding her pups, there were several places of worship including the Red Lion and the Butt Hole.

Formerly known blandly as the Brewery Tap this tavern was so nicknamed after a sprot who infiltrated the town, drank himself in to a stupor on Stefan Neumann's fine ales and, becoming over friendly with the staff, was finally chased away by the landlady, Neumann's wife Juanita, wielding a red hot poker which allegedly did far more than just singe the miscreant. Apparently he didn't hang around long enough to sample the treatment at the state of the art Conisbrough Hospital.

As we've said the townsfolk mainly worked the land, played a role in the militia that protected the dynasty from nasty surprises or worked the local treacle mines at Denaby and Cadeby. Paxman Conisbrough, youngest son of His Lordship Padraig Conisbrough was based at the castle and had overall responsibility for the management of the treacle operations in Yorkshire and Derbyshire. In effect he was Ayrton Speckmeister's boss and he wasn't happy: any loss or theft of treacle was taken very seriously. Although there was the odd incident of unruly behaviour in Chesterflood there had been no theft and the last reported crime in Conisbrough was the landlady's assault on the drunken sprot which the militia wrote off as self defence.

Paxman had asked Speckmeister to come to Yorkshire and meet with him and his father for he had been unsure of Speckmeister's culpability in the loss of the five sacks of treacle. His Lordship pointed out to Paxman that the Speckmeisters had been loyal employees for almost two hundred years without an incident of this nature. Although young and inexperienced, Ayrton (unlike some of the curmudgeonly earlier generations) had shown enthusiasm for his work and his working relationship with Conisbrough. When Ayrton had left the meeting, having convincingly offered his explanation, Lord Conisbrough indicated to Paxman that he thought Speckmeister innocent of any wrongdoing but nevertheless wanted Paxman to get to the bottom of the issue. The clue for Lord Conisbrough came when Speckmeister entered the meeting room and promptly sat down in the coal scuttle.

Part of Glass

So Paxman returned to Chesterflood in the week following armed with a number of options agreed with His Lordship. While in Chesterflood Paxman would stay in his dedicated quarters at the very same tavern in which Henny was lodging. It was a comfortable establishment that provided guests and employees alike with shelter from the inclement weather experienced (it wasn't called Chesterflood for nothing) as it was one of the few buildings in the town to have glass windows instead of the draughty wooden slats to which most had become accustomed.

Although far from what we are used to today the Conisbroughs had begun production of small quantities of glass using silicates from Lincolnshire and metals mined in Northamptonshire. One of Paxman's nephews, Pilkington Conisbrough had established a small factory further down the River Con. This was a far from ideal location at this time given the presence of a number of impurities in the water they drew from the Con. While Stefan Neumann drew his water for his beer making before it reached Sprot, Pilkington had no such good fortune. That said, he produced enough material for Conisbrough Castle, the taverns in the town and, selfishly we suppose, those places like the Chesterflood tavern where Conisbroughs had to do business.

The Sedition of the Magician

Never let it be said that the members of the dynasty were all perfect, sweetness and light for they were far from that. During that time when parts of continental Europe were under English rule Patrick Conisbrough who was in charge of the supply of treacle to Essex and the eastern counties changed his name back to Con against family wishes and causing disrespect to the Brough family. Lord Conisbrough moved the prodigal son to Belgium where initially he fared well supplying family treacle to the local monks to assist them in their beer making (now you know why it tastes so bad) but inexplicably he lost the contract when undercut by Brussels sprots selling the monks a cheap chemical alternative.

Fortunately this was a temporary setback to the operation (though Patrick never regained what reputation he had). Cranbourne, Lanbourne (His Lordship's Chief Negotiators) intervened and soon established that the sprot placebo failed local emissions tests and the monks turned again to the dynasty for their sugary wares. It was at this stage that Dieter Dangelhosen was brought in to replace the flakey and increasingly irrational and error prone Patrick. The Dangelhosens from Cologne in Germany were related to the Conisbroughs through several marriages and business interests.

It was after one of these marriage ceremonies – attended by Lord Conisbrough, his son Palmerston and Conisbrough's younger brother Paxman, the High Sheriff of Billericay – that the party's ship got in to difficulties in mid channel and was wrecked off the Isle of Wight. Conisbrough's squire, Higson, became very agitated as their ship floundered claiming that he had been told stories by his father and grandfather (both of whom had been in service with the Conisbroughs) that the island was mystical and inhabited by flesh eating sprots. Fortunately only part of the story was true for as the ship broke up and the party was forced in to the swell near the Needles none of them was hurt or became the slightest bit wet.

Unbeknown to all members of the party the Isle of Wight was uninhabited with one or two noteworthy exceptions. The flaky and error prone Patrick Conisbrough and his fellow traveller, Miranda Masala had been similarly washed up on the magic island some days earlier while Patrick was attempting to steal unnoticed back to England. If we reported that the chance meeting between Patrick, his father, his uncle and younger brother ended in reconciliation and renewed back slapping bonhomie we would be fibbing. It turned out more like an episode of Blackadder or one of those Brian Rix farces with people running everywhere, hiding in laundry baskets with their trousers falling down – and that was just Higson. The magical island seemed to possess them all except Miranda Masala, Patrick's cook. To this day the Isle of Wight has a similar effect on many visitors.

Miranda had grown tired of Patrick's mewling and groaning about his misfortune in Belgium; here it was ten times worse and getting progressively more intolerable as the days passed and their diet drawn from the local snake and rabbit population dwindled. Word had it that back in Brussels Miranda could perform wonders with a snake but here, on a God forsaken uninhabited island, the joke was wearing a bit thin. For Miranda, living with Patrick for weeks had been bad enough but now she had to contend with the jittery Higson who was seeing ghosts and ghouls behind every tree trunk and, what she described as, the rest of Patrick's worthless layabout family. After preparing supper Miranda decided to walk alone to the far north of the island. Halfway to the coastline on a hillside in the middle of the island light from ships and houses was everywhere to be seen just a few miles away across a channel.

To be fair to Miranda she appreciated that this was not the Conisbroughs' finest hour. We can understand her frustration with the inconsistent Patrick but, surely, for the rest of the party such indolence and stupidity was completely out of character. There was, to her way of thinking, something about this island that was driving them all nuts. The sooner they made their escape the better. The worrying thing for Miranda was she was convinced she could see another light after she left the hillside. Approaching carefully she saw what appeared to be a blonde woman, clearly a sophisticated lady, running in her direction and wearing a silver sequinned dress, pursued by what at first glance appeared to be a maniacal creature which cackled and giggled like a demented goose but turned out to be a man pulling playing cards from the undergrowth. Rubbing her eyes and thinking she'd had quite enough of this place she hastily made her way back to the Conisbrough camp.

Either way, heartened by the knowledge that salvation lay across the Solent, the following morning the dishevelled group made their way across the island and, in exchange for Lord Conisbrough's Rolex, a sprot prawn fisherman ferried them to the mainland. Miranda would never fully understand why Patrick continually muttered that a wizard called Paul Daniels, a magician, sex symbol and bodybuilder and his beautiful wife Debbie McGee were practising their evil form of witchcraft on the island – but she suspected it had something to do with her vision the evening before. Patrick spent the rest of his days in a sanatorium near Huddersfield and not a day went by without him regaling the staff and other patients with his stories of Paul Daniels and the amazing Debbie McGee.

The Insight of the Eyesight

Back in Chesterflood Henny and her children, Sharon and Andrew, had settled in to a small house provided by the Council near Josephine Speckmeister's home. It may have been small but such was Henny's pride and delight at having her own home (with a roof that kept out the constant rain) that she had soon transformed it in to one of the most attractive houses on the street with its own flower garden, vegetable patch and with herbs growing around her kitchen window so she could take in the marvellous aroma. It would have been nice if Ayrton Speckmeister had been able to see it for himself rather than relying on his mother's word but, sadly, he couldn't.

Her food stall positively flourished in this busy environment and soon she approached the Council about taking over a redundant building near the Conisbrough treacle storage tanks that she wished to convert in to another food outlet. Henny spoke to Josephine about putting her doughnuts on display and offered a position to Speckmeister's sister Jenny who, having completed her education was eager to take on new challenges. The Council agreed and Henny and Jenny set about renovating what realistically amounted to little more than a small dilapidated storage space. It was not worth inviting Ayrton to help them as he had his own duties to attend to and doubtless would have trouble finding the exact location.

It was a surprise to him then when Jenny Speckmeister came bounding into his office begging him to come and help them. Even Ayrton couldn't fail to see the broad grin on Jenny's face as he accompanied her across Chesterflood to the new Hotbox premises. He had a smile of his own when, entering the building he tripped on the five sacks of missing treacle. It would appear Ayrton, when moving freshly mined treacle from a cart to the holding tanks had merely dropped them in the wrong place and the disused store room had kept the secret all those weeks.

While Ayrton and Jenny danced for joy, at that moment Henny's recollection of Paxman Conisbrough through the window of the tavern gave her the spark of an idea that was to put Chesterflood on the map for reasons other than treacle, incessant rain and Josephine's doughnuts. Her first sight of Paxman Conisbrough at the tavern came through the glass window of the taproom where the young man was enjoying his supper when Henny returned from the market. He had looked very short and stout but entering the bar area her eyes had deceived as she met a tall imposing man with a svelte figure and snake like hips. Eureka – glass could change what one could see.

To cut a long story short, and once the missing treacle issue had been resolved, Henny, now known to Paxman for her part in finding the treacle sacks, approached Paxman for some glass samples from Pilkington as she felt she now had more than the germ of an idea that might not only change Ayrton's life but the lives of thousands. In keeping with the Conisbrough philosophy Paxman embraced the entrepreneurial spirit of the young woman. Samples were delivered and, slowly but surely, Henny with assistance from Conisbrough physicists and chemists, produced some rudimentary eye glasses for Ayrton. The results were astonishing. Henny became known as "The Speck Saviour" and from that day forward she concentrated on her new business venture which is still well known today apparently. Her fast food outlets were left in the capable hands of Jenny and Josephine whose doughnuts received even more exposure with being sold alongside the full Hotbox range.

Love's Labour's Lost

We know that you wanted Henny and Ayrton to get it together. Or perhaps Henny and Paxman? Unfortunately this is a true historical account and not one of those stories with contrived and nonsensical happy endings. One suspects that Henny had no interest in forming any romantic or any other kind of relationship and devoted herself to providing the north of the kingdom with better eyesight. Her children and grandchildren would be relied upon to carry on her good work and the Hotbox name. Ayrton, his sight restored, married a local girl called Avengia. Their children would remain in the area with differing levels of success and the eldest Speckmeister son would remain in employ with the dynasty to this day.

With his new eyeglasses Ayrton never again lost track of dynasty treacle and was only summoned before Lord Conisbrough once more to receive a long service medal and the gift of his own home near the treacle mine at Staveley. At the age of 45 he was able to leave his mother's home at last. His professional activity was only disrupted when he took off his eye glasses and, predictably, couldn't find where he had put them down. This gave Henny and the Pilkington scientists something to work on but it would be a few centuries before the contact lens would be invented and available in the south of the kingdom.

Part Two

Part Two

Description of the Conscription

In the 16th century the Conisbroughs continued to go from strength to strength. As had been the case for a number of centuries the dynasty was largely left to its own devices. This was due in no small part to its power and influence – and even reigning monarchs saw it as advantageous to support the loyal dynasty rather than do anything to upset the status quo. The dynasty frequently gave back and the tale of Palmerston Conisbrough, third son of Lord Padraig and Lady Gaga, is a classic example. He attended the Court of Queen Bessie the Benevolent who formed quite a liking and attraction for the younger man to the extent that he (and by dint the dynasty) was presented with additional lands and a home. Palmerston first met the monarch at a masked ball where she expressed a liking for his pleasing disposition and handsome appearance. He went to live in the home bestowed on him at Broad Green near the present day Wellingborough. The dynasty already had substantial properties in Northamptonshire but the mining operations were solely iron ore and some coal with treacle in very short supply. Nevertheless the area was bustling and profitable. Palmerston was successively made Lord of the Manor of

Wellingborough, Lord Lieutenant of Northamptonshire and Lord Chancellor of England by the grateful monarch.

It's not entirely clear what he did to earn such titles, power and reputation for himself and the dynasty. Word has it his elder brothers were slightly jealous and put out by the success and notoriety of their sibling. We have attempted to obtain more flesh on the bone from the Conisbrough's own historical records but, it is alleged, these were destroyed in a road accident involving the present day Lady Geek Geek who managed to spin the family Volkswagen through 90 degrees while doing 180mph – or perhaps it was the other way round. Either way we are not satisfied with the explanation and believe sordid (or at least saucy) details are being withheld from the reader. It can't have been anything bad as his head stayed attached to his shoulders – more than can be said of some courtiers who came in to contact with Bessie. One senses that her given title "Benevolent" is either a historical error or an early example of Sprot humour.

We digress and are jumping forward a few centuries but it's worth mentioning a few details of Lady Geek Geek's road accident that we were able to glean from the police report. The officer attending the scene found Her Ladyship and a young man half her age unresponsive and unconscious so they were taken to hospital where happily both made a speedy recovery. It turned out the young man was Lady Geek Geek's personal fitness trainer so that solves that riddle and dispels rumours of impropriety. But the accident investigator, slightly bewildered at the cause while surveying the scene, was interrupted by a monkey clambering over the wreckage of the Passat.

"I wish you could talk" said the officer at which the monkey shook his head up and down vigorously. "Can you understand what I'm saying?" asked the officer and again the monkey nodded. "Did you see what happened?" enquired the officer. The monkey indicated he had and made a pouring gesture with his paw. "They were drinking?" and the monkey confirmed it and then made as if he were smoking a cigarette and then wobbled a little. "And they were smoking marijuana as well? Anything else?". The monkey puckered up his lips and pretended to be cuddling himself. "How do you know all this?" asked the officer. The monkey made a driving motion with an imaginary steering wheel.

The matter might have gone further but for the fact the monkey ran off (doubtless fearing three points on his licence). A small quantity of an illegal substance was found in the car together with an empty bottle of Bollinger but, somehow, the drugs were lost in the Sergeant's office at Romford Police Station before any sort of prosecution could be mounted. To our knowledge Lord Padraig knows only the barest details and let's hope it stays that way.

School for Scoundrel

At this time most Conisbrough boys were educated at Urmston Grammar School founded by Sir Richard Urmston. Urmston, in common with the Neumann and Conisbrough families, had been a member of the Worshipful Company of Brewers and was Lord Mayor of the City of London in 1544. After Urmston's death in 1556 his will decreed the founding of a school for boys in Oindle in Northamptonshire, close to where Palmerston would make his home.

The size and reputation of Urmston Grammar School rose steadily in the following years such that many of the school's pupils had been sent from all parts of England and beyond. The decision was made to divide the school into Oindle School and Urmston Grammar School. Urmston Grammar School would continue to educate local boys while Oindle School was to accept only the sons of gentlemen from further afield. It is during this period that Oindle rose to prominence as an English Public School, which can be largely attributed to Simon Barrett in his role as headmaster from 1592 until his death in 1622. When Barrett joined Oindle he found a minor country boarding school, by the time of his death the school had become the leading establishment for science and engineering education. The success of Barrett can be attributed to his educational ethos; he believed in teaching students what they wanted to learn and as a result helped to introduce subjects such as science, modern languages, and engineering to the English independent school system.

Such a free-thinking philosophy fitted perfectly with the Conisbrough requirement though Barrett was to find himself in trouble with the local Labour Party for his policy of discriminating against sprot boys who he banned from admission – although to be fair many disqualified themselves through sheer ignorance during the entrance examinations.

As punishment for his behaviour Barrett was placed in the stocks in the village and boys of Urmston Grammar School (some of whom were sprots) were invited to throw stale Melton Mowbray pork pies at the white haired academic. Not only did he lose his dignity but it is said he also lost a tooth attempting to munch on one of the reviled flying comestibles though, privately, many supported his stance. The local Labour Party leader soon got his comeuppance when Barrett and the Conisbroughs alerted the constabulary to his tendency to hold orgies in Oindle attended by eager sprot juveniles.

Girls Just Wanna Have Fun

Another younger Conisbrough joined the Royal Guard at the palace for a number of years and there is a record of correspondence with Lord Padraig and Lady Gaga on the subject which we reproduce below:-

My Dear Mother and Father

I am very well, I hope you are too. Tell big brothers Padraig, Patrick and Palmerston that the Queen's Guard is better than working for the family; tell them to get into the Guards quick before the jobs are all gone.

I was a bit slow settling down at first because you don't get out of bed until 6am, but I got used to it and I like sleeping in now. All you do before breakfast is make your bed, shine your boots and clean your uniform. No cows to milk, no calves to feed, no treacle to stack, nothing. Men must shave, but it's not too bad because there's hot water and plenty of candlelight to see what you're doing. For breakfast there's cereal, fruit and eggs but there's no fillet steaks or sausages. You don't get fed again until noon, and by that time all the town boys in my platoon are buggered because we've been on a 'route march', which is just like walking to the well in the meadow.

This will kill Padraig and Palmerston with laughter but I keep getting medals for shooting!! I don't know why because the bulls-eye is as big as a bloody bull's head and it doesn't move and it's not firing back at you like the sprots did when our bull got their cow in calf before the Irchester show. All you have to do is make yourself comfortable and hit the target – piece of cake. You don't even load your own musket as a squire manages everything and you don't have to steady yourself against the roll bar of the treacle extractor when you reload. Sometimes we wrestle with the town boys and I have to be very careful because they break easily – it's not like fighting with Padraig, Patrick and Palmerston and all the other local sprots all at once like we do.

It turns out I'm not bad at unarmed combat either; it looks like I'm the best the platoon's got. I've only been beaten once by this guy from Chesterflood – he's 6 foot 8 and 20 stone so he's a good bit bigger than me but I fought to the end.

I can't complain about the Guards – tell the boys to get in quick before word gets out how good it is.

Your loving daughter,

Patricia

The Ghost of Higson's Passed

The Conisbroughs weren't big on portraits – those enormous life sized paintings that you see on the staircases of stately homes, castles and the like. They did make a point of sitting for family group portraits on rare occasions but when we say rare we mean once, possibly twice a generation, and the artist was required to make them as small as possible. Visitors to Conisbrough Castle were slightly surprised at the lack of art but successive generations had preferred to adorn the halls and staircases with tapestries, rugs, the odd shield or chunk of armour and great vases of fresh flowers.

One person who must have been secretly pleased by this policy was Higson. Generations of the Higson family had served as squire and housekeeper to the dynasty at the castle. Mrs Higson was rarely on view as her duties were below stairs in charge of the kitchens and the ranks of maids who scurried around performing their various duties. Under normal circumstances Higson would have been delighted with this as his accommodation (and his supply of fine wine) was above stairs on one of the upper floors.

After a dinner party at the castle Higson had completed his duties in the drawing rooms and after extinguishing all the candles on the ground floor was making his way up the staircases when a woman in a nightgown appeared before him. Accounts of how this happened vary dramatically. Higson swore on his wife's life that the woman had come through the wall on the staircase adjacent to one of the very few family portraits hanging there. Others say that Higson had cleared the drawing room of the castle by draining every last glass of their contents of mead, wine, port, ale and several blends of whisky and that it wouldn't have come as a surprise to many if Higson had reported seeing a three headed sprot with eight legs.

That said Higson was found shivering and shaking early the next morning in exactly the same spot by a slightly bewildered maid carrying wood for the fires. Mrs Higson was woken and her ashen husband was taken below stairs out of the way of the Conisbroughs and served a hot treacle drink with a dash of brandy. Higson could barely bring himself to recall his vision such was his state of anxiety. After another couple of Mrs Higson's treacle specials the petrified squire was feeling a little more relaxed and was taken to his rooms where he might rest.

In the history of the dynasty one statistic worth mentioning was that no Higson had ever taken time off work or even been a minute late responding to an instruction. Consequently Higson was missed when Lord and Lady Conisbrough took breakfast. Their server blurted out that Higson had seen a ghost and had been forced to retire to his rooms. Ordinarily such a pronouncement from one of the castle staff would have had little impact on Lord and Lady Conisbrough but strangely they both exchanged glances and looked concerned – as opposed to worried – according to observers.

When he had regained his accustomed wit and some poise Higson appeared before Lord Padraig who asked him not to explain his absence from his duties but the detail of what he had observed. Higson did his best to recall exactly the circumstances and not what he had told the kitchen staff after four brandies. It felt slightly odd that His Lordship asked him which direction the young woman had travelled in once reaching the foot of the stairs and the time as best as Higson could recall. It was even more bizarre to Higson when Lord Conisbrough accompanied him to the exact spot on the staircase without any need for Higson to direct him.

Hardly able to look at the wall and certainly not the family painting Higson confirmed the precise step where the young woman had emerged and what she had looked like. Lord Padraig asked Higson if a woman he was pointing to in the family portrait was the vision he had seen. Barely able to bring himself to look Higson felt sick and weak when the young woman he had observed stared back at him from the artwork, albeit dressed in riding gear as opposed to a white nightgown.

Returning to Lord Padraig's study and pouring a large brandy for them both, His Lordship provided his theory on what had occurred. Many years earlier the young woman in the picture, Peggy Conisbrough, had been struck by lightning and killed late at night out in the meadows. Last evening had been the anniversary of the tragic accident. It was too much of a coincidence for Lord Padraig to ignore as Higson saw her moments before the lightning struck all those years before. It was Lord Padraig's hope that the young woman's spirit meant no harm to anyone but merely wanted to rejoin the frivolity she had been pursuing on that fateful night.

Lord Conisbrough advised Higson to remove the family portrait and place it in store. Higson, demonstrating a sensitivity and awareness that rarely surfaced during the course of his official duties, asked that Lady Peggy be allowed to remain where she was, undisturbed and, indeed, commemorated by the family of which she had been such a keen part. Higson offered to record the circumstances so that no repetition of his experience would be witnessed by another member of staff, the Conisbroughs or their guests. Higson's son, who had been concerned for his father's health, was in training as a squire with Master Patrick, and would hopefully inherit his father's position and would be told of events and the agreed solution.

On the anniversary of Lady Peggy's midnight stroll Higson would ensure there was no member of staff above stairs and the family and any visitors would be advised of the occasion and invited to allow Lady Peggy her adventure undisturbed. It is impossible to prove one way or the other whether Higson's idea worked as Peggy's peace was respected. There remains to this day a rumour that on the anniversary and before retiring Higson placed a tankard of Neumann ale at the foot of the staircase. Apparently the beer had been drained when the tankard was collected the following morning and nobody has ever claimed to have drunk it.

The remaining question surrounding this mystery is that the family portrait went missing during castle renovations many years and several generations later. Nothing has been heard of Lady Peggy since but hopefully she is still with us (alive and well wouldn't be the appropriate phrase) and enjoying an annual stroll. Should you encounter her our suggestion would be to offer her a glass of decent beer and not a golf club. If you find your beer glass emptied in strange circumstances late into the night Lady Peggy could be closer than you think...

The New Model Barmy

The 17th century brought more turmoil and internal strife to the kingdom than the Black Death before it and the Conisbroughs of the period had to play this one particularly carefully or risk losing substantial assets and influence.

For many years religious tolerance had obtained not only within the dynasty but throughout the kingdom. While Bessie the Benevolent had tried and failed to maintain the status quo her successor Jimmy Topman had achieved that elusive balance by preserving Protestant doctrine within an essentially Catholic structure. When he was succeeded as King by Charlie Scaffold, a protestant who promptly married a Catholic girl, it was hoped that this was a signal that the coexistence could be maintained. Sadly not, for Charlie had too high an opinion of himself and fell out big style with his own Parliament and MPs while frittering money away and imposing unhelpful and unfair taxation to cover his debts.

King Charlie came to visit the Conisbroughs at their house in Nottingham in 1642 to discuss his future plans. The meeting didn't go well and the Conisbrough party left Nottingham in the night to return to the castle. The next day, doubtless in frustration that one of the most valued friends of the Royal Court had shunned his proposals, Charlie effectively declared war on his own people, raised the Royal Standard over Nottingham Castle and ordered dynasty treacle to be forfeit and sold to raise money for weapons and men to wage the war. When his Royal Standard blew down in a storm and was last seen floating down the River Trent this was seen by all as a very bad omen indeed.

Charlie attempted to build bridges with Lord Padraig by visiting again shortly after and in an attempt to raise an army. Nobody from Conisbrough joined his force as the vast majority of men had work in the mines or tending the harvests and would not leave their families on a fool's errand. Consequently Charlie ended up with an army of volunteer sprots eager for the promised wages and regular meals. Apart from being a collection of boorish, arrogant, drunk, womanising, conceited oafs they would serve the King well.

Although they had little time for one another because he frequently stood in the way of Conisbrough expansion plans, Oliver Crimewave, the MP for Cambridge and self-appointed opposition to the monarchy, and Padraig Conisbrough had a grudging respect for one another. After Crimewave and his army commanders had won the first skirmishes with Charlie's elite sprot army he came to visit Conisbrough on the pretence of recruiting for his own force, the New Model Army. A few members of the local militia did indeed join him believing in the causes of freedom, a democratic Parliament and an end to the tyranny espoused by Charlie. But this was more about persuading Conisbrough to command, a request that was politely declined.

History records that it was left to Sir Thomas Filofax to take command of the armies under Crimewave. Unfortunately for the dynasty Crimewave also appointed a Colonel Alexander Ayresome to be second in command to Filofax in the north. Ayresome, who was known as the Thornaby Demon for his tendency to worship pagan Norse Gods at midnight wearing female undergarments, was indeed a thorn in the side of the dynasty. For generations the Ayresome family had prevented the dynasty from expanding north of York and, while the internal conflict raged, the Conisbrough dynasty had no intention of risking further resources.

The Instigation
of the Restoration

This terrible period in the history of the kingdom went on too long and while not decimating the population in the same way as disease had centuries earlier still had a huge impact on the numbers of working age males. Once again this offered the dynasty an opportunity but the expansion of the business empire would have to wait and the Conisbroughs kept their profile low until the position changed. As the armed conflict petered out and turned in to a political conflict instead many families which had been friends and allies of the dynasty for generations were now diametrically opposed. Similarly, especially in the south where the Conisbroughs were relatively unknown apart from their support for the university at Willesden, a number of established families looked to form new partnerships with the dynasty.

One such family were the Lambournes of Andover. Percy Lambourne had made no secret of his loyalty to the royal family – not through blind faith but more out of principled opposition to what he regarded as an oafish unsophisticated leader in Oliver Crimewave. Sir Percy had kept it remarkably quiet that he was supplying arms to both warring factions from his factory on Salisbury Plain and emerged from the conflict unscathed, knighted and a very rich man. His own enlightened and highly-developed tastes drew him in to business with the dynasty through the purchase of ales for the many taverns that sprang up on his land, as well as small quantities of treacle which when mixed with oil proved an excellent lubricant for Sir Percy's range of muskets, howitzers and other assorted missiles.

It was during a courtesy visit to the Lambournes that the then Patrick Conisbrough agreed to purchase some land from a neighbour of the Lambournes who had fallen on hard times following the conflict. So commenced the dynasty's first mining operations in what we today call the south. The end of armed conflict had reduced the outputs from Lambourne's munitions factory and spare labour eagerly took up the offer of employment in the mining industry. The same mutually beneficial business relationship proved less easy to develop with landowners to the east.

The Grand Old Dork of York

But we get ahead of ourselves. The Civil War ended in a most unpredictable way. Crimewave had been in poor health for some time, severely hampered by a battle wound he had received shortly before the conflict died down. His temper would not have been improved had he known that it was one of Percy's musket balls which had penetrated his breeches and lodged itself in his right buttock.

Command and the title Lord Protector passed to his son, Essex. While the name Essex Crimewave will remain with us until modern times the same could not be said of the new Lord Protector who was a weak and vacillating individual devoid of all personality or sense. The tiresome Ayresome, rallied and encouraged by his supporters across Scotland and the northern counties, marched on London hoping to seize power for himself while this vacuum existed. Unfortunately he had a number of sprot guides in his party and it took the Ayresome army two months to reach the outskirts of London by which time a new king had arrived in the country and the mood had changed completely. After a bit of sightseeing Ayresome turned around and plodded back towards York.

On his return, tired, penniless and utterly disenchanted with life, Ayresome had to urgently find a fresh source of income. In his absence his so-called friends, filthy, kilt-wearing, two-faced and ginger haired wildlings from further north who had encouraged his sortie south were looking to expand their own sphere of influence. Ayresome rightly felt under threat and sent a trusted friend, Kenny Mealing, south to meet the Conisbroughs and effectively buy their help. With this the Conisbroughs were able to expand their business interests beyond Yorkshire to the north for the first time, taking advantage of significant mining opportunities and an eager labour force, for families had been on the brink of poverty following Ayresome's ridiculous venture to London.

Sadly for the Ayresomes from being one of the most powerful families in the north they fell in to total obscurity. Present day members of this once proud line occupy lowly blue collar positions and count passing the Cycling Proficiency Test as the family's main achievement since 1660. Alexander Ayresome did seek bigger and better things and, deserting his family and his own kind, spent some months as elected Mayor of Berwick on Tweed. Unfortunately he was caught *in flagrante delecto* with a sprot boy, a pig, a packet of marshmallows and a box of firelighters by Conisbrough appointed militia. While such practices were legal two hundred yards away across the border he was sentenced to a term in the local jail where he became the girlfriend of two renowned Scottish poets and authors, Phil McAvity and Willie Stroker, who were serving jail terms for seditious writing and overuse of outrageous puns.

The Brothers were Grim

It was around about this time that the union of the Conisbrough and Dangelhosen families became closer and firmer. There had been significant trade over the years during periods when international exchanges usually meant cavalry charges and the families had inter married on a few occasions. For three hundred years Conisbrough had been exporting treacle to the Dangelhosens and other businesses in northern Germany every three months or so, often in difficult circumstances. The standard process was for the product to be loaded on ships in Conisbrough to the mouth of the Con, across the North Sea to the Rhine estuary and then south east towards Cologne. Irrespective of whether their countries were on good terms at the time or not (usually not) the business partnerships and friendships flourished.

It was normal practice for members of the militia to travel with the cargo in case of difficulty with robbers, bandits or the like. If members of the Conisbrough family were travelling then the route might change and more time spent journeying overland so other family and business connections could be visited. Often the Conisbrough guards would only come as far as the coast where the Dangelhosens would provide an escort for the onward journey. Much would depend on who was travelling and where they were living so the route, while pre-planned, was flexible.

Lord Padraig Conisbrough was accompanying his son Palmerston along with Higson and several cousins from the south of England for Palmerston's marriage to Ingrid Dangelhosen. Palmerston was to remain in Germany with Ingrid to explore local mining opportunities with the Dangelhosens. It had been the Conisbrough view for some time that there were treacle deposits in northern Germany that should be explored. With Dangelhosen support and Conisbrough expertise a fresh industry could be established. Cranbourne Lanbourne would ensure a healthy profit came back to the dynasty.

It was normal practice for the hosts to meet the Conisbrough party and send approximately three escorts for every guest expected but, despite there being eight people in the group on this occasion only two guards, brothers in the Dangelhosen militia, had turned up to meet them. Fortunately members of the group spoke German as the brothers could speak not a word of English.

They explained in translation that the escort party had been attacked on the road and many of their group had suffered injuries which made it impossible for them to continue. The brothers had such thick armour and helmets that they had escaped harm and had been able to chase the attackers off but were strangely reticent when asked to describe their adversaries, and their number and strength, so the party could be prepared should they seek to intercept again. The brothers said that they would be taking a different route so as to avoid any repetition.

Lord Conisbrough said that was not possible as lack of time before the scheduled wedding ceremony meant a direct route was essential. Thinking on his feet and taking advice from Higson (who had travelled this route very frequently) and the Head of the Conisbrough militia, Lord Padraig decided that even if it meant leaving things thin back at Conisbrough three guards, while exhausted and relatively inexperienced, would accompany them. Thus they had five armed guards, seven family members capable of defending themselves – but lightly armed and with no battle protection – and Higson.

In fact Higson with his better than passable German proved to be of most value finally eliciting from the taciturn brothers from Dangelhosen that they were slightly embarrassed by their ambushers who had descended on them just before dawn while they still slept. Higson translated the description they provided in German as "trolls" which sent the party in to something of a spin as, although few people claimed to have seen these woodland creatures, stories of their aggression abounded.

Higson said that there was nothing to worry about so long as they were careful as trolls were nocturnal and their skin burnt badly on coming into contact with daylight. They would travel hard during the day and take shelter in a town or village at night where they would be better able to protect themselves. As a group of thirteen people (all with horse) including Higson driving the armoured cart they should be able to manage. Setting off the three young members of His Lordship's guard looked even more terrified than their German counterparts.

The journey should have taken no more than three days but there had been severe storms in the area and, warned the Dangelhosen contingent, a river bridge had been badly damaged leaving it doubtful that the cart would be able to cross until repairs had been completed. Lord Conisbrough asserted that they would not divert but see what could be done on arrival. In fact the bridge was not too badly damaged at all and the Conisbrough party repeated their view that the brothers wanted to take a different road because of the frightening attack that they had experienced. Nobody could entirely blame them.

In the event slow but steady progress was made and shelter taken on the first two nights in taverns in small towns with two guards staying on duty with the cart and horses in three hour periods. The day before they were due to reach Dangelhosen's castle near Cologne a thunderstorm with heavy rains and lightning stopped the group in its tracks. The cart became stuck and the horses were too spooked to assist in dragging it free. There was nothing for it but to wait out the storm and begin the final part of the journey the following morning. There was a woodcutter's hut that provided some relief from the deluge but it was not big enough for the group to sleep in except in shifts.

At this point, as everyone looked to everyone else for guidance, Higson started barking orders. Six of the group were to shelter in the hut and rest as best they could while six would stay on guard inside the cart which, although stuck fast, was both watertight and secure from attack. Higson said he would remain on top of the wagon underneath sheeting acting as lookout with all the muskets loaded and dry under the empty baskets of supplies brought for the journey. Lord Conisbrough and Palmerston thought briefly about protesting but let Higson get on with it.

Near dawn when the group was in a half sleep but beginning to shiver from their damp clothes there was such an almighty din from outside the hut near the cart that all thought they had been transported to a battlefield. Seeing movement and glowing eyes approaching the cart Higson had remained quiet until he saw a small shadowy outline before discharging his musket. Lord Conisbrough's squire didn't wait to see what happened but reached for the second and third loaded firearm. Engineered by the Lambournes in their factory near Andover we'll never know what damage Higson caused with his volley of shot from his trusty muskets but the skirmish ended abruptly and, so they alleged, before the guards within the cart had been able to join Higson's action against their enemy.

Whatever it was, or whoever they were, fled the scene and only as dawn broke did Higson venture down from his vantage point and instruct the rest of the party to join him believing the situation sufficiently safe. The group scoured the surrounding area but found no bodies only pools of greenish fluid that must have been caused by Higson's close range musket fire. Higson's claim that he had killed twelve beasts while only firing five times was a source of some amusement to the group and the story is still told to this day to Dangelhosen children who want to venture too far into the woods.

Higson suggested that the beasts had carried away their own dead and wounded and would be feasting on their flesh now in one of their caves. Better their flesh than ours was the group consensus. The brothers from Dangelhosen asked Higson how he knew so much about the ways and methods of trolls. The squire replied that he is constantly reminded by Mrs Higson that she has been married to one for thirty years.

Heidi-Hi, Ho-Di-Ho

The remainder of the visit and the return journey were unremarkable in comparison but no less exciting. Before the party set off back to England, this time down river to the coast rather than overland, there was much to discuss and much to do. The marriage between Palmerston and Ingrid was to take place the following day; and a hastily arranged ceremony to honour and reward the brothers from the Dangelhosen guard, the injured members of the group who had to return to the castle after the first encounter with the trolls and the still traumatised recruits from the Conisbrough militia.

Graf Dangelhosen, on receiving the report of what took place from the brothers, wanted to ensure that Higson's role in the skirmish (although he was not a member of the guard) was properly recognised and celebrated too. Higson was the hero and everyone wanted him to tell his story over and over. Unfortunately for his eager, enthusiastic and petrified audiences the story changed each time – possibly coinciding with the quantity of hospitality the squire consumed. By the time he had finished regaling his worshippers with the story the trolls had grown to twice the size of a horse, there had been a whole army of them and Higson had engaged the attackers in hand-to-hand combat rather than firing from the roof of an armoured cart.

Nobody, especially his hosts and Lord Padraig, wanted to spoil the fun Higson and, to be truthful, everyone else was having – out of sheer relief, if nothing else. One little girl called Heidi, the daughter of one of the brothers, having listened to Higson's first account of his combat actions, held his hand throughout that day never leaving his side. Presumably her equally grateful father had told the child of how Higson had saved the group from attack, but her devotion to Higson while charming seemed slightly unusual.

In a quiet moment between storytelling and watching Higson demolish roast pork and potatoes, Heidi whispered to Higson that she knew how to stop trolls too. As Heidi was no more than seven or eight years old Higson, even with a potentially more stimulating group to socialise with, was not the type of man to be the least dismissive of this delightful child and her stories. Talking at such a fast pace the squire barely understood so Heidi ran off and minutes later returned with one of her dolls.

Heidi explained that her brother made dolls so lifelike that from even a short distance away you couldn't tell it wasn't a human child. It was Heidi's job to make little clothes for her toy and play with it as only little girls can. But what Heidi said next both amazed and startled Higson and, for a brief moment he was face to face with a scary creature, as opposed to events as they unfolded in his storytelling. The child explained that trolls prefer eating babies and children to grownups as their flesh is sweeter. Caught slightly off-guard by Heidi's candour and knowledge of the subject Higson begged her to go on.

Heidi explained that the previous year she had been

playing alone with one of her dolls – most likely too far in the woods too late in the evening for her father's liking – when confronted by a troll which, ignoring Heidi had made off with her doll. Her explanation, which Higson found utterly compelling and plausible, was that the troll thought her lifelike doll was a baby and the doll's "abduction" had probably saved her own life. Heidi added that she found her doll the next morning discarded undamaged by the abductor. Since that time she had placed a number of her dolls in the woods and had then taken cover and watched what happened. On each occasion, at nightfall, a troll had come, sniffed the doll and had taken it away some distance before dropping it.

Schenkt Ein, Trinkt Aus! (I poured you one so drink it!)

The Dangelhosens lived in a magnificent house in seemingly endless grounds at Solingen, a few miles from the centre of present day Cologne, surrounded by lakes and forests. Successive Conisbroughs had always felt at home there as it reminded them of the Con Valley on a slightly grander scale but without the castle and abbey. The local church was the ideal spot for a wedding and the celebration went off without a hitch. As was traditional in Graf Dangelhosen's family the happy couple disappeared after the ceremony for their honeymoon and their guests returned to the house for a banquet to honour Ingrid and Palmerston. In a display of generosity and inclusivity that was pure Conisbrough Higson and Lord Padraig's guards were invited to the function as special guests.

While Higson was familiar with such grand occasions, if only from the other side of the table so to speak, the young guards – all of whom had suitable clothes provided to them for such an occasion – looked as petrified as the first time they were told about the trolls as they experienced what would probably be the opportunity of a lifetime. It had been Heidi's idea, obviously tiring of just dressing her dolls that

Higson should wear white shirt, knee length leather trousers with colourful braces, long socks and heavy clogs topped off with a feather cap. "Why not?" had been the gist of Higson's response as he took his place at table with the young guards, including the brothers from the Dangelhosen militia.

It was only halfway through the feast, as Graf Dangelhosen proceeded to call people forward to receive applause for their bravery, that Higson and His Lordship became aware that the two brothers were the Graf's nephews. The Conisbrough guards received a small gold figurine each and summoning Higson forward (with Heidi holding his hand, of course) presented him with the same and what his host described as a special and unique commemoration. Higson's smile took on a distinctly false appearance and he shivered just a little when he was handed a hastily commissioned portrait of himself and a subdued sixteen foot troll.

Invited to speak Higson first lifted Heidi on to the nearest table and then proceeded to clamber up and thank his hosts for their hospitality. It had been an error on the part of the Graf to hand Higson a massive stein of ale for the speech. Ten minutes later and still speaking but barely standing Higson must have thanked everyone in the room – even though it was them thanking him. He had made a particular serious point about Heidi's ruse to defeat the trolls with her lifelike dolls and the audience gave the smiling child her own rapturous applause.

By the time Higson, swaying like a candle's flame caught in a breeze, was helped down he had arranged for the Graf's nephews to return to Conisbrough for training and experience with "his" militia and had put forward proposals that would see the bewildered Conisbrough guards stay on in Solingen too. We suspect Lord Padraig might have taken slight offence at his squire's going far beyond his remit but His Lordship, along with the rest of the assembled guests, had tears of laughter rolling down their cheeks at the sight of Higson in his shorts with a stein half his size and with Heidi still clinging to his free hand.

From that day forward a life-size lifelike doll was strapped to the saddle of anyone travelling during darkness; likewise dolls were placed on the sides of wagons, often dressed in real infant clothes that the original owner had outgrown but still retained the unique smell of a baby. There were countless reports of trolls sneaking up and snatching these toys but, for the first time in Dangelhosen memory, the town of Solingen had suffered no casualties. Sadly the same could not be said for sprot villages further down the valley which had failed to embrace change and new technology.

The Confusion of the Infusion

For hundreds of years the dynasty had been obtaining hops from the east where it had a number of business interests including one of the first oil wells ever developed in the kingdom. The main suppliers, running a sort of workers' co-operative, were gentlemen and landowners called Nettleham and Holton and the areas of peak production of the finest hops and barley were between Lincoln and Habrough which was to the north of the county. The Nettleham family were rather impolitely described as grocers by the then Lady Gaw Gaw who tended to say what she thought when she had had a couple of glasses of port.

In fact they were far from it having developed extremely sophisticated ways of rewarding employees based on production and profit. The Nettlehams' land produced some of the finest hops in Europe – a fact that hadn't escaped the attention of the Neumann brewing contingent and those Conisbroughs sober enough to appreciate the fact. Their neighbours to the north the Holtons grew high yielding barley (as the soil was perfectly suited and the climate was mild and as wet as Chesterflood) and raised hunting dogs.

Following the Civil War the price of their hops and barley almost trebled. The accountants who had managed dynasty affairs for donkey's years gasped at the increase and set about exploring less expensive suppliers. There were plenty offering their product at the pre-war prices but the brewers were reluctant to accept second best. So Archibald Cranbourne sought a meeting with Holton and Nettleham to endeavour to establish the rationale behind the price hike. In fact the sneaky Cranbourne met both men separately without advising the other of his intention.

Both Holton and Nettleham claimed the other had forced him in to raising the price because the dynasty had failed to take their side during the Civil War conflict and they would only do business at the new rate. The fact that nobody knew which side they were on further confused the issue when Cranbourne reported back to His Lordship. Holton also convinced Nettleham that men in Lord Conisbrough's employ were responsible for the Great Fire of Spondon when the premises of one of Nettleham's suppliers near Derby were razed to the ground. The fact that Lord Conisbrough had purchased a fire engine for the village many years earlier and had nothing whatsoever to do with the incident was lost on them.

Such flights of fancy and imagination were all too common when dealing with people from Lincolnshire. Nettleham lived in a pretty village that bore his name and where generations before him had been raised. The village was idyllic with a green and small lake at its centre fed by a babbling brook that ran down the main street. The tree lined roads were all awash with colour from the many flower beds of wild and cultivated plants and shrubs. In spring the scent was overpowering. Interestingly there was no tavern and consequently no sprots were ever attracted to the area. The perfect beauty and tranquillity of the village and surrounds meant the Baron and his family rarely ventured far. It was possibly this inability to visit and comprehend the real world that made Nettleham behave the way he did for he trusted nobody outside his immediate circle.

The Holtons were essentially farmers and had obtained title many generations earlier when the area had been invaded by Normans. For reasons that history has not recorded King Willy of Normandy knighted the then Dick Holton and presented him with a gift of some dogs for an apparent show of loyalty. Some say that the Holtons had become informers for the Northern French invaders and advised where the resistance leaders lived; others said that the new King merely took pity on Holton because he was so ugly he could easily be mistaken for a Norman. Given that modern day Holtons have not improved in the looks department we prefer the latter explanation suspecting generations of inter breeding had caused such a calamity. The Holtons would do exactly what the Nettlehams told them to do.

Consulting his master brewers Lord Conisbrough set up a plan that he hoped would eventually force concessions from Nettleham and Holton. While barley grows very rapidly hops take a considerable amount of time to establish so the brewers obtained mature plants from Germany (albeit at significant cost) and planted these along with the barley on the small tracts of land that the dynasty controlled in the general area. Sadly oil exploration was postponed but it would prove lucrative in years to come. The workers designated to other tasks were deployed to hop and barley cultivation under the supervision of the brewers initially and their wages were calculated to match those of the now rival growers.

While the overall quality and quantity took some years to raise to previously enjoyed levels the objective was achieved and Nettleham and Holton, neither of whom had budged an inch on the issue, lost fortunes as their main customer had not only ignored them but had persuaded most other brewers to do the same. Nettleham slowly but surely went out of business completely and sold his lands in the Lincoln area and retreated to his village. Holton fared slightly better but his reputation in the industry had been shattered. He continued to supply grain to sprot bakers in Market Rasen but the majority of his land was bought from him cheaply and turned in to a racecourse. He and his family continued to breed and raise dogs though his methods would bring him to the attention of the authorities on numerous occasions.

Early Modern Post Modernism

At the beginning of the 18th century there were a number of events that could have ruined the Conisbroughs. The dynasty's usually cautious approach was tested to the extreme during a time of great expansion, modernisation and social development. The established monarchy had sought out the Conisbroughs, with their now vast business and property interests stretching countrywide, to assist in implementing unification of the various parts of the kingdom that had hitherto been allowed to remain separate. With Cranbourne Lanbourne Ripoff and Scarper in the lead the dynasty assisted Parliament in the drafting of an Act of Union. Scots and sprots alike railed at the prospect but, as remains the case today, sprots were financially and morally bankrupt and needed the kingdom and the dynasty to help them out of their precarious monetary Armageddon caused by years of over-indulgence and a propensity to not pay for anything they could steal.

But the focus of this period was the extension of the range of business around the globe. The Conisbroughs resisted the temptation to jump on this gravy train but became heavily involved in ship building for both the expanding Royal Navy and the various companies that were trading in the Americas and the Far East. In the south Sir Horatio Lambourne re-opened the family munitions factory to satisfy the need for naval guns and equipment for public and private sectors alike. It was truly the beginning of the British Empire. Such activity in commerce, industry and the financial sector which made millions for some and made monkeys out of millions, was something similar to the strategy practised by the Conisbrough dynasty for eight hundred years.

The South Bermondsey Bubble

The South Bermondsey Company was established by Cranbourne Lanbourne Ripoff and Scarper and not, as history recorded, by the Conisbroughs. Sensing an opportunity to renegotiate high-interest paying government loans in exchange for granting trading licences across the globe which, incidentally, Cranbourne Lanbourne knew precious little about apart from what was in the newspapers, a limited company was established by the oily, self-aggrandising Lanbourne. Some of the countries for which the devilish Cranbourne Lanbourne sold licences had only just been discovered by intrepid adventurers and proper understanding of the trading opportunities, risks and rewards barely existed at the time.

By the time Cranbourne Lanbourne sold on their final licences to a consortium of Millwall supporters who wanted to establish a penal colony in a place called Australia they had multiplied their investment to the power of ten and had retreated to their offices near Holborn to count their money. Of course, Cranbourne Lanbourne were not responsible for the fact that 95% of the licences were worthless but speculators kept driving the paper value higher until, months later, reality dawned and hundreds of greedy sprots lost their life savings and were made bankrupt. The South Bermondsey bubble had well and truly burst.

Fortunately and ironically the penal colony in Australia was a winner and many of the sprots who had invested in the illusion and promise of wealth found themselves onboard Conisbrough-built ships following deportation to the prison colony on Van Godforsaken Land Island off the Australian coast. The speculators who proved winners from this particular venture formed a gentleman's sports club with the profits and Millwall Association Football Club exists to this day and is at the very top of its sport with matches attended by local ladies and gentlemen.

The mainly sprot cargo that frequently plied a human trade between England and Australia has a substantial community in present day Tasmania. Nobody can explain why dart boards manufactured there have small images of Cranbourne and Lanbourne instead of the traditional red and green bull's eye. We doubt Cranbourne Lanbourne lose sleep over this opportunity in which they played a blinder and they remain the most respected and financially secure firm of lawyers and accountants according to their brochure.

Vindaloo and Waterloo

At the turn of the century the now United Kingdom was challenged once again by France – more of a contest of ideologies than a dispute over territory, religion or politics. The Conisbroughs understood this well, the dynasty having fought an ideological battle against enemies in their own country since they settled in Con generations earlier. The Conisbroughs never supported conflict and throughout the ages had done all they could to avoid it – with considerable success. The dynasty regarded it as wasteful and pointless, much like religion or worse still, religious intolerance.

This philosophy did not prevent some recent members of the dynasty from taking an active role in a struggle when they felt the kingdom, and with it the dynasty, was under threat. One such occasion was when Napoleon Sprotapart, who was running amuck in most of Europe and had sequestered land from the Dangelhosens, threatened to bring his vast sprot armies across the English Channel out of nothing more than jealousy of what the kingdom had achieved in science, trade and colonial expansion. We strongly suspect that he perceived the sprots in the kingdom had been persecuted for hundreds of years and wanted to redress the balance. As with most sprot plans this one not only never got off the ground but failed to even stand up.

Arthur Wellesley Conisbrough, while fresh out of Oindle School, along with a number of his more belligerent siblings and cousins, felt disgusted at the prospect of Napoleon Sprotapart threatening the dynasty. Worse still their cousins Helmut and Titiana Dangelhosen had had their ancestral home near Cologne seized by Sprotapart's army and converted in to a gentleman's club for the benefit of the army officers and selected toadying hangers on. Arthur had spent many a happy summer holiday playing with Titiana in the grounds and, with the image of Sprotapart now roaming the welcoming passages, felt compelled to act.

After rapid and accelerated training at the Lambourne's military academy in Andover Arthur was sent to assist in the campaign in India where a local troublemaker and Sprotapart supporter, Tipsy Sultansprot, was disrupting the trade in exotic spices, cottons and hideous fatal diseases. Arthur, with only a small brigade, drove Tipsy out of the area at the battle of Vindaloo. Following this success Arthur was promoted rapidly following a string of successful engagements in the conflict with Napoleon Sprotapart.

Soon commanding the entire force Arthur Wellesley Conisbrough weakened his adversary so fatally that defeat at the Battle of Waterloo put paid to war and misery in Europe for at least eighteen months. Now granted the title the Duke of Willington (a charming spot between Derby and Burton with a redundant power station) this member of the Conisbrough dynasty rose to become one of the most acclaimed politicians and ambassadors to the benefit of the kingdom. Whether Arthur could see the "big picture" or not remains a mystery and is not revealed in his memoirs or letters but we feel he did, possessing that prescience we spoke of much earlier that was a Conisbrough trait.

You see with the defeat of Napoleon Sprotapart the entire European map was redrawn and the terrible cost borne by the supporters of Sprotapart meant that their hold and influence on world trade was dismantled. Re-establishing themselves quickly in Cologne the Dangelhosens demonstrated to the kingdom and the dynasty how they could benefit from the trading void that existed and that fresh negotiations with previously hostile partners was possible. During the next few years the dynasty's wealth through trade would become considerable, almost rivalling the Cranbourne Lanbourne balance sheet.

The Conisbroughs and a few others embraced the change that the 19th century brought with it. While the Dangelhosens in Germany paved the way for a new dynasty there, the Conisbroughs were well placed to take full advantage of the change in the shape of the world map and the rapidly accelerating pace of scientific discovery closer to home. The Conisbrough clinics and teaching hospitals had been at the forefront of medical pioneering since the onset of the Black Death, their sponsorship of educational development through the first university of its kind at Willesden, at Oindle School and in all towns and villages where they had interests.

Riding Hood and the Wolf

We wouldn't want you to think that as we meandered through the Conisbrough generations that we had forgotten to provide detail of the real power behind the dynasty. No, not Cranbourne Lanbourne, but Her Ladyship. This novel covers the period from 1016 until the present day. There have been thirteen Lord Padraigs on our journey from the time Padraig Con married Lady Gee Gee of Brough to sow the seeds of the Conisbrough dynasty and, remarkably, thirteen have married and enjoyed children. As the fourteenth Lord Conisbrough we're not sure whether the present incumbent is feeling like going on for another thousand years.

While all Lady Conisbroughs made their mark in one shape or form there are two or three examples of exceptional or amusing actions that typify the Conisbrough spirit (and we don't mean brandy). One such event occurred in the very early years of the 16th century shortly after Lord Padraig had succeeded his father and married Lady Grace Gu Gu. Prior to their marriage Grace had joined the militia in Conisbrough and had impressed her superior officers with her bravery in skirmishes with sprots and her calm nature in dealing with difficult situations in the locality. As nominal commanding officer of the security force Lord Padraig came to hear of this young woman's fortitude.

On one occasion Lord Padraig was travelling back to

Conisbrough accompanied by senior members of his close protection team when the group was intercepted by a team of militia lead by Grace Gu Gu who advised that there had been reports of a wild animal, possibly a wolf, in the woodland bordering Sprot. Padraig was knocked off his feet by her beauty and bearing as her command accompanied the main group safely in to the village and back up to the castle before heading back out to cover more ground in what would prove a vain search for the beast.

After a short courtship Padraig and Grace were married in Conisbrough Abbey but not until this single minded young woman had put down a number of markers which, predictably, were agreed by her new husband. First, she was to assume command of the militia and not Padraig who, frankly, needed little persuading; secondly, and rather more difficult to digest for the besotted Padraig, she was to remain an active member of the militia ceding command to the duty officer when in action; thirdly, flatly refused by Padraig until he spotted the twinkle in Gu Gu's eye, Grace insisted their first child be named Boadicea.

Some months later, while strolling through the village on their way to a meeting, Padraig and Grace were alerted to fresh reports of the beast seen attempting to cross the River Con with a sprot in its mouth. The fortunate sprot had wriggled free, probably released by the beast due it tasting so dreadful, and reporting to the other citizens of Sprot word was reluctantly passed to the militia. Sprot only cooperated with the Conisbrough guards when their own interests were at stake but, on this occasion, the threat was clearly real on both banks of the river.

The sprot involved in the abduction was indeed badly scratched and claimed he had been carried off not by the jaws of a snarling wolf but by a unicorn. He insisted that the elusive beast (which was seen on a regular basis by one self-obsessed narcissistic attention-seeking sprot after another) could only be captured if it was persuaded to fall asleep in the lap of a virgin. That ruled out anyone over the age of 13 in Sprot. Lady Grace saw the sprot's wounds and firmly believed it to be a wolf that had developed a taste for human flesh – albeit putrefacting pustule ridden flesh, which tended to suggest the wolf was very hungry.

Lady Grace took it upon herself, with some help from Padraig's squire, Higson, to trap the animal rather than butcher it and then release it far to the north in the Badlands where it could roam and find quarry without bothering any human neighbours. At first the sprot was reluctant to act as bait for the trap but, once he realised that Lady Grace was teasing him, eagerly suggested a number of his fellow sprots who he believed should be tied to trees to entice the beast into a trap. Lady Grace had formulated another idea which involved digging a pit into which a cage could be lowered. Once the beast fell in to the trap the door would spring shut.

With the carpentry skills developed over many years Higson created the bars of the cage out of willow and lashed them together in a hole dug by the sprots. Lady Grace placed some roast lamb in the cage and then had the pit covered with branches so the beast would be following its nose at the scent and not watching exactly where it was going. After a few false starts when sprots fell into the pit and devoured the beast's meal the group on watch finally had success. The wolf, barely an adult, looked less ferocious behind bars but all knew it posed a real threat if it were allowed to coexist with the communities of Sprot and Conisbrough. Lady Grace insisted that she and four trusted recruits accompany the beast to the Badlands where it would be released.

Stories spread of the beast turning and bowing to Lady Grace when it was released in gratitude at her having spared its life rather than just skewering it and throwing it on a sprot barbecue. Others say that the wolf returns to Conisbrough on the anniversary of its release from captivity to call out to Her Ladyship. For her part Grace laughed on hearing this and said the howling was Higson having a nightmare about falling in a vat of ale. But such was the twinkling magic in this young woman's eyes it would be easy to imagine otherwise.

Lady Grace Gu Gu was to go down in Conisbrough history as the wolf huntress. Whether out of respect, admiration, commemoration or self aggrandisement we know not but from that day forward the bowing wolf featured on the Conisbrough crest and was the emblem of the militia across Yorkshire and Derbyshire. Lady Grace outlived her husband and when finally reunited with him in the grounds of the Abbey those present all witnessed a family of wolves running through the woods on the hillside near the castle. They were never seen again but the story lives on.

It Will All End in Tears

The ninth Lord Padraig of Conisbrough, living in an age when Protestants, Catholics and non-believers were all beating hell out of one another in the name of God, was not (in common with previous Lord Conisbroughs) a big fan of the abbot or Conisbrough Abbey but Grace had asked to join her husband, his father, overlooking the Con Valley. Although he knew his mother was a spiritual and Christian woman he had never known her talk or spout religion nor was he aware she had ever attended services at the abbey.

It came as something of a surprise when the Abbot asked if he might share in Lady Grace's eulogy. What this apparent stranger – who evidently knew Grace very well indeed and better than many related to her – had to say sent the mourners away in floods of tears but smiling from ear to ear.

The abbot's eulogy went something like this "When God created Lady Grace he had to work late and an angel came by and asked "Why spend so much time on her?" The Lord answered. "Have you seen all the specifications I have to meet to make this one? She must function in all kinds of situations; she must be able to embrace many children at the same time, have a hug that can heal anything from a bruised knee to a broken heart and she must do all this with only two hands. She cures herself when sick and can work all the hours in the day".

Impressed the angel asked if all women such as this are created in this way. The Lord replied yes but I think this one might be extra special as I'm in a hearty mood today. The angel came closer and touched the woman. "But you have made her so soft, Lord". "She is soft", said the Lord, "but I have made her strong. You can't imagine what she will be able to endure and overcome"

"Can she think for herself?" The angel asked and The Lord answered. "Not only can she think, she can reason and negotiate." The Angel touched her cheeks. "Lord, it seems this creation is leaking! You have put too many burdens on her." "She is not leaking…it is but a tear and tears are her way of expressing her grief, her doubts, her love, her loneliness, her suffering and her pride."

This made a big impression on the angel, "Lord, you are a genius. You thought of everything. This woman is indeed marvellous."

The abbot then spoke his own words. "Grace had the strength of two men, handled all manner of burdens with a smile on her face – even when she felt like screaming. She held senior positions, opinions, happiness and love. She sang when she should have cried and laughed when afraid. She fought for what she believed in.

Her love was unconditional. Her heart was broken when a relative or a friend died but she finds strength to get on with life. Grace was far from perfect because she constantly forgot what she was worth to those around her".

A Better Life for Me and You

We have observed that, despite the obvious temptation and some encouragement, successive Lord Conisbroughs had been able to steer a course wide of religion, political friction and taking sides in national and international conflicts. Our view, not that you're remotely interested in what we think, is that the dynasty has been all the more successful, moral and corruption-free as a consequence. The eleventh Lord Padraig whose position as head of the dynasty covered the Victorian era might have proved the exception had it not been for the timely intervention of his wife Lady Gertrude Gab Gab.

Although they will surely deny the obvious and defend the indefensible, it is our view (as independent observers with no axe to grind against the sycophantic dullard fossils Cranbourne Lanbourne), that his Lordship was given bad advice. That's all very well for as we all know you don't have to take bad advice – especially if it stares you in the face and flies contrary to most dynasty principles. It's not as if Cranbourne Lanbourne had proved a constant source of bad advice for the reverse usually applied. A contemporary commentator, who did have a bit of an axe to grind against the Conisbroughs, said of dynasty integrity that "it was like a soggy ginger biscuit, dunked for too long in the tea of our expectations, and now crumbling and dissolving into nothingness". In our view, with germane and succinct comments like this, Charles Dickens might have had a future as a writer.

Shortly after assuming control from his late father in 1815 Lord Padraig, perhaps feeling overshadowed by his uncles Arthur Wellesley Conisbrough and Charles Darwin Conisbrough, and acting on advice from Cranbourne Lanbourne, established the "Organisation for a Better Life". It sounds innocent enough but the philanthropic message hid some sinister and dark secrets. Lady Gab Gab, feeling this was not something to which she could sign up, established her own foundation to actively support Conisbrough family members and affiliated families in their many and varied projects at this exciting time in history. George Stephenson Conisbrough was undertaking work on steam driven engines; David Brewster Pilkington-Hotbox, a descendant of Henny Hotbox, was marketing newly invented micro- and kaleidoscopes; and Faraday Conisbrough was making progress with what we know as electricity.

Meanwhile His Lordship's "Organisation for a Better Life" had set about buying up independent newspaper companies, large tracts of farm land –ostensibly for mining and drilling purposes – and building roads and carriageways across the country wherever they could. So what's wrong with all that, we hear you say? Well, first, all those independent newspaper companies started speaking the same language and delivering the same message – much more spiritual than usual, perhaps bigoted is a better word, with warning messages for those that might support unions and workers' rights. This must have seemed bizarre to contemporary observers as the Conisbroughs had traditionally valued their employees like members of their family; a free and independent press had been at the heart of their ideology; and the dynasty had rarely purchased land for the sake of it or, as seemed likely in this instance, to stop someone else from owning it and making a living on it.

The Man in the Dry Castle

At this time, but certainly not acting on advice from Cranbourne Lanbourne, His Lordship declared himself to be teetotal and banned all alcohol from Conisbrough Castle. Judging by the newspaper editorials of the time he'd have liked to have extended his regulation to the village but, mercifully for Lanbourne – still a regular in the Butt Hole like his ancestors before him – His Lordship's zeal was curtailed in the nick of time.

Higson was the obvious one to suffer as he had built up an impressive collection of wines and spirits which he partook of with gusto. He was instructed to remove the offending bottles together with all the contents of the Conisbrough cellars which His Lordship said should be smashed. You can count on the fingers of one hand how many times down the years a Higson has ignored an instruction from a Conisbrough but this was one occasion. Unable to persuade Padraig to preserve and mothball the cellars for the benefit of future generations Higson, waiting for Lord Conisbrough to leave for a meeting with newly appointed cronies at Conisbrough Hospital, carted the priceless collection down to the brewery.

Once Neumann's pride and joy the brewery's beer production had been severely impacted by the New Conisbrough Policy (or NCP, as it was known sneeringly to the locals) and was now almost exclusively engaged in bottling a variety of Conisbrough branded spring and mineral waters along with seltzers, potions and fluids that were supposed to make you feel better. In truth, had the customers known the ingredients in some of these medicaments they would have winced – that is if they'd had time to wince before developing the severest and fatal of convulsions.

But at least the brewery's store rooms were now put to good use as Higson and Lanbourne (undertaking manual labour for the first and last time in his life) unloaded the bottles from the creaking cart and stacked them lovingly on the empty shelves where once barrels of Neumann's foaming ales had briefly stood before being transferred to an eager audience next door. Lanbourne provided a lock for the store so the contents would be safe but Higson refused to believe that Lanbourne only had one key. Threatening to spill the beans to His Lordship the odious Lanbourne, almost incontinent with anticipation at the sampling experiments he could undertake, somehow produced a duplicate. The collection was safe. Some months later when the wines took the return journey Lanbourne was again on hand to assist; not this time with the hard labour but by taking a glass or three from each vintage to ensure it had survived the journey up and down the hill in its former condition.

Higson was also instructed to arrange for the conversion of the cellar – an original part of the castle building – in to a family chapel with meeting rooms for his friends in the Round Table and local Conservative Party Association. While Higson did not on this occasion ignore the instruction his request to local sprot building company Bodged and

Dodged met with a hand slapped to a forehead and a promise to complete the work by the following spring on payment of the full amount in advance.

Profess to Confess

Charles Dickens's short stories and serialised novels were all spiked by the various Conisbrough newspaper editors to whom he submitted his work. These Conisbrough-manipulated editors were under strict instruction to omit anything flowery, romantic or effete preferring punchy headlines about strike breaking and erosion of management prerogative. Lady Gab Gab looked on in horror as all this was happening; powerless to influence her husband who seemed to her hypnotised in to unravelling all the Conisbroughs had stood for. Few Lady Conisbroughs were shrinking violets and Gertrude Gab Gab was no exception plotting (though we prefer devising) a way out of this spell under which her beloved husband had fallen. It would take her a number of months but, against a background when a woman's role in society was being redefined – and not for the better – she eventually succeeded.

The catalyst to success was a doctor His Lordship had appointed to Conisbrough Hospital. Professor Acton Yard was a self-acclaimed expert in women's health. On visiting Yard for a routine check up Lady Gertrude was staggered when advised by the mealy mouthed medic that she should spend more time at home looking after the children and not attempt to usurp Lord Padraig's natural intellectual and commercial superiority. Acton went on to say that too much business activity had a damaging effect on the ovaries and would turn Her Ladyship into a dried up old prune. Let it be said that Lady Gertrude at approaching six feet tall with shoulder length flame red hair and skin as soft as on the bottoms of her two young children was far from being in the running to win a "dried up old prune" prize at the County Show.

Staggered at Acton Yard's bombastic patronising tones she somehow kept her cool and invited him to continue with his sage advice. It got better. Acton warned Her Ladyship that he had heard of her being "forward" in the company of men (we think talking to a man or group of men at a business meeting would have qualified as forward in Yard's eyes). He said that he believed Her Ladyship to have a worrying sexual appetite and suggested a number of potions that he believed would cure her lust. Yard said that, happily, a number of women to whom he had prescribed his (outrageously expensive) draught medicaments are no longer troubled with sexual feeling of any kind.

Seething inside but retaining a calm exterior Lady Gertrude enquired of Acton whether their conversation was confidential. Of course, Her Ladyship knew it wouldn't be but wondered where the information would go. Gertrude, drawing on acting skills perfected years earlier in her school plays, broke down in tears thanking Acton for being so easy to talk to and having such a perfect understanding of the minds and ways of women. Lady Gertrude then admitted that she had been unfaithful and had contracted syphilis while enjoying sexual adventures and other drunken debauchery with a troupe of travelling sprot circus performers. She made sure to detail the special abilities that one particular trapeze artist brought to the party while upside down.

Eyes bulging and face redder than blood Acton Yard could barely contain his indignation. Failing to provide any medicines, advice or suggest further appointments Yard could not have ushered Her Ladyship from his plush offices any quicker. It was as if he expected her to stain the rug at any moment or worse still come within touching distance. Despite her pleading for help Yard slammed the door on Her Ladyship and, racing back to his desk as fast as his stubby legs could carry him, reached for pen and ink.

Her Ladyship couldn't help but giggle and give herself a little clap at her performance but she realised or, at least, suspected that the more serious stuff was yet to come. We don't wish to dwell in this true account of the Conisbroughs on unpleasant dealings between Lord Padraig and Her Ladyship for over the course of a thousand years there have been precious few. Unfortunately this was not one of the happier moments on the Conisbrough timeline.

The Effrontery of Adultery

On his return from a business trip the following day Lord Padraig summoned Lady Gab Gab to his rooms. For her part Her Ladyship was prepared. She made Higson stand outside the study door threatening to tell everybody where he kept his sherry stashed away if he refused. He didn't refuse. Lord Conisbrough announced to Her Ladyship that he would be applying to the Court in Chesterflood for a divorce. The grounds, he went on to say, were adultery and disease. Lady Gertrude, flatly denying the assertion and protesting complete innocence, enquired what conceivable evidence could there be against her. The case was being assembled by Cranbourne Lanbourne apparently.

Her Ladyship warned that such an allegation was an affront to her and her family and that she and the children would not budge from the Castle while such preposterous allegations were unproven. She went on to say that if His Lordship insisted on pursuing this ridiculous course she would be obliged to counter sue for defamation and divorce on the grounds of unreasonable behaviour; and would be seeking 50% of the Conisbrough lands, wealth and other assets. His Lordship blanched slightly at the thought – pulling much the same face as when Lanbourne had farted at a recent dinner party shortly after the cheese had been served.

We're going on a bit but we think it's important to record in some depth. Suffice to say the source of the allegation was never cited. The proceedings were established and respected independently appointed medical examiners reported that Lady Gertrude was not possessed of any disease transmitted by sexual activity. This undermined half the petition but fortunately, when somehow the allegations had hit the presses of numerous newspapers not yet owned by Lord Conisbrough, seventy three sprot trapeze artists had come forward to own up to the dastardly deed of giving Her Ladyship a good tupping – not that they would have been interested in the reward on offer for information that would assist.

Painstakingly, while racking up mountainous fees, Cranbourne Lanbourne countering the petition from Her Ladyship's lawyers interviewed all the sprots who claimed to be the miscreant. None could describe Her Ladyship in the slightest detail, nor select her from a number of drawings that had been provided. This left Cranbourne Lanbourne scratching their dry scalps. Reluctantly they recommended to His Lordship that he instruct them to withdraw the divorce petition in its current form and invite Her Ladyship's lawyers to do the same.

With Lady Gertrude's innocence now staring him in the face Lord Padraig was, above all other things, embarrassed, for he remained deeply in love with Her Ladyship but had felt forced to act in the way he did by those around him rather than doing things the Conisbrough way and using his instincts and judgement. He went down on one knee in front of Her Ladyship as he had when proposing marriage some six years earlier and begged forgiveness (we heard this from Higson who was stationed outside the door again).

There were conditions. Her Ladyship suggested that this whole matter, costing thousands, could have been avoided if he listened to her a little more and to his experts and cronies slightly less. She asked that he consider dropping his involvement in the Organisation for a Better Life as she felt its aims and objectives were not Conisbrough-friendly; and she suggested that Beaverbrook Conisbrough, a cousin showing some promise in this new industry, be invited to assume control of the Conisbrough media empire. Having come to his senses Lord Padraig agreed. Nobody knows what happened to Professor Acton Yard but he left the hospital without as much as a goodbye to anyone taking only his books on the study of female medicine. A rumour circulated that he was struck by a carriage carrying a troupe of sprot circus performers and was forced to retire. Apparently a wheel of the carriage had run over and crushed certain parts of his lower abdomen. He had from that day forward been unable to do little more than squeak instead of speak.

Out of the Mouths of Babes

One final example – this time rather more amusing and not involving divorce petitions or fierce wild animals – involved Lady Gaga back in the late 16th century. Lady Gaga had four children, Padraig, Patrick, Palmerston and Patricia (no surprises there) but as she and indeed Lord Padraig were approaching old age they had only one grandchild. Predictably the couple were devoted to the little chap (who would go on to manage the dynasty during the turbulent times of the Civil War) and were often slightly over protective.

Lady Gaga was out walking with Master Padraig in the town's market when he picked up a piece of fruit from the ground and promptly sent it in the direction of his mouth. "If you don't mind, I'll have that" said Lady Gaga, much to the bemusement of her young grandson. You could imagine him thinking that if he found it his Grandmother shouldn't take it and eat it herself. "Why?" came the response we will all be familiar with. "Because it has been on the ground in a market where people and animals have been walking. You don't know where it came from and it probably has germs that could make little boys called Padraig very unwell".

Rather than arguing with his grandmother the young Padraig looked up at her in complete admiration and said

"How do you know so many things, Grandmother? You are the cleverest person I know". Lady Gaga responded that she was not particularly smart but all grandmothers have to pass a test after learning such things and only then are they allowed out with their grandchildren. A nearby stallholder on seeing and hearing this episode unfold smilingly handed young Padraig a plum which, on receiving a nod of assent from Gaga, he sucked on as they walked on.

The silence was broken when Junior Padraig asked what happened to people who didn't pass the test. Her Ladyship replied "Well they just have to settle for being grandfathers." Young Padraig seemed happy with this clarification – as indeed we all should be.

Animal, Vegetable
or Miracle?

One member of the Conisbrough dynasty who their hospital was unable to save was Charles Darwin Conisbrough who suffered from heart problems, stomach pains and stress throughout his life. They kept him going though and Charles Darwin Conisbrough achieved much before his passing aged 73. Nowadays he is celebrated as one of the most influential individuals to have ever lived. One of his famous quotations was," It is not the strongest of the species that survive, nor the most intelligent, but the one most responsive to change".

No Conisbrough had been sufficiently erudite to express that sentiment but, as you will doubtless have gleaned by now, it was a principle by which the dynasty lived and developed since the earliest days. It was Charles Darwin's passion and legacy to make this thinking popular belief as opposed to being the province of the enlightened or the crazy – depending on your perspective. How he achieved this, by smashing the theory of the creation and replacing it with the origin of the species was so groundbreaking it took some time (to put it mildly) for it to permeate through society.

The Church proved a major and powerful opponent of

the theory as believers in the Books of Genesis and Exodus burnt copies of Charles's findings and reports when they should have been consigning Adam and Eve to the library's fiction section (albeit one of the best written and enduring books of all time).

The dynasty lost a number of friends during this time because, except for that very brief period that was more of an aberration on the part of His Lordship, it refused to accept the strict social "norms" regarding modesty and gender roles. Lady Gertrude had seen to that – and Lady Grace before her would have been unable to conform such was her spirit of adventure and independence. Perhaps following some sort of odd fashion, many of the Conisbroughs' friends found the Victorian era spiritually and morally uplifting marking a return to decency, propriety and clean living. While it might have sounded arrogant to some Lord Conisbrough, usually at dinner parties when the wine was flowing, declared that he had no need to return to those values as they had been core to his family's very existence for seven hundred years.

The Brightside of Life

On one occasion, when one of their guests had been accompanied by a young black boy, no more than twelve or thirteen, who was clearly a product of some disgusting and despicable slave trade from earlier years, Lord Conisbrough – a different man from the one who had been taken in by Acton Yard and his cronies – made clear his disgust (that had been shared by his father and grandfather) with the enslavement of other human beings. His guests, the Member of Parliament for Sheffield and his wife, argued that there had been no other way to run our plantations in the West Indies than to recruit labour from elsewhere.

The Right Honourable Member for Sheffield went on to say we lived in changing times and the future prosperity of the nation was at stake. Keeping his cool remarkably well Lord Padraig said that recruiting people to work for you implied they had a degree of choice. By way of an example he compared the situation with the houseboy, who Padraig wagered had had no choice in his placement with the Member, with the situation of a number of families and individuals in the locality (even some across the water in Sprot) who had settled voluntarily and out of choice. There were Europeans from Germany, Spain and Italy; families from Asia and the Far East who had ended up here following involvement in legitimate trade in treacle, spices, cotton and precious stones. There were a few black families who had doubtless been released from whatever appalling contracts they had with their virtuous and grateful employers.

Padraig said that a descendant of the cook of one of his ancestors worked in the castle kitchens under Mrs Higson. Murgh Masala, so named because he had excruciatingly thin and white legs like an anaemic chicken, was free to come and go (and he frequently did) unlike their black boy. Our Right Honourable Friend said his houseboy was free to go at any time and had said he preferred living with the member's family to anything else in the world. Latching on to this Padraig said that the assembled guests could all leave now. Alternatively they could stay, enjoy the rest of the dinner on condition that their houseboy remain in Conisbrough for a month. Higson would accompany them back to Sheffield in the morning; serve as their butler for a month; while the boy remained here allocated various tasks by Mrs Higson.

His Lordship continued. At the end of one calendar month the boy alone would decide which existence he preferred. If he chose a life in Sheffield so be it Lord Conisbrough was wrong on all counts; he would compensate the Member to the tune of one thousand guineas. As this was a small fortune there was a splutter and choking sound from the end of the table where Lanbourne had been innocently ignoring the debate while demolishing three of Mrs Higson's raspberry pavlovas, washing them down with a variety of dessert wines that had somehow appeared next to him on the dinner table. The discussion having turned to a subject closer to his heart than even Mrs Higson's cooking saw the accountant burst in to life.

The Right Honourable Gentleman was in a corner of his own making having, for no other reason than decoration, brought a young boy from Sheffield to Conisbrough to stand in a corner and pick up his napkin when it fell from his grasp. Unable to resist Conisbrough's wager the plan was agreed. The Member for Sheffield asked whether Higson would be content with the arrangement and His Lordship replied that he would follow instructions as, unlike the houseboy, he was well rewarded for his trouble. Padraig added that he would meet the houseboy's salary too – at which point there was a painful silence.

Lanbourne meanwhile, and rapidly catching up with the conversation, had rather liked the idea of having another servant and asked if he might assist while the boy was staying with them. In truth the houseboy had been most attentive to Lanbourne during the meal by providing him with fresh napkins and removing those discarded, drenched in sweat, by the obese accountant. Padraig agreed provided the boy was paid a salary at which Lanbourne shook his head almost choking on a large plum he had attempted to consume in one gulp. Her Ladyship patted Lanbourne on the back to relieve his discomfort while thinking it should have been her husband's back she was patting.

There is a Sheffield Far Away

You can all guess how this ended. Whereas sprots continued to employ children at this time schools under the auspices of the Conisbrough dynasty obliged families to send their children to learn at least five subjects until they were fifteen. Then the children and their parents might decide whether the individual child was suited to further education often based on advice from tutors or one of dozens of apprenticeships run by Conisbrough and suited to the industries and operations at that time. Indeed this had been the Conisbrough philosophy and policy for as long as anyone could remember, had worked well, benefitted all and had passed the test of time. So the boy – who said his name was Abraham – went to school in Conisbrough and only worked with Mrs Higson in the afternoon. Abraham took his meals with the staff except on weekends when Lord and Lady Conisbrough took him for a meal at the tavern. Nobody batted an eyelid as convention was not something rigorously followed by anyone in Conisbrough.

One or two eyebrows were raised at Lanbourne who, failing to persuade the ever smiling Abraham to buy him a glass of Bordeaux in the Butt Hole, had suggested Abraham might benefit from additional private tuition in mathematics and European Literature which he and Cranbourne would be delighted to provide if the boy could find a sponsor to pay their ridiculous teaching fees. Growling at Lanbourne Her Ladyship needed no words to convince the egregious accountant to provide his services pro bono.

At the end of one month Higson returned in remarkably good spirits commenting that his temporary host's wine cellar had been remarkably impressive and his duties had been light and straightforward. One suspected from his cheery disposition that he was either thrilled at being reunited with Mrs Higson or, unlikely we know, had spent his spare time in Sheffield collecting tankard-sized souvenirs. Abraham, via Padraig, had politely made his preference to remain in Conisbrough by letter to our Right Honourable friend who, nagged by his wife and children, had to hastily employ an expensive local butler recommended by Higson who had, by chance, met this individual strolling between the Fat Cat in Alma Street and the White Hart in Russell Street in Sheffield.

In fact Abraham had escaped Conisbrough before the end of his allotted month – not running from the chains of servitude but invited to accompany His Lordship and other family members on a little tour that Dieter Dangelhosen had put together. Against the wishes of the government of the day and advice from Cranbourne Lanbourne they were to visit St Petersburg at the invitation of a number of prominent families there. The British Empire now accounted for around 20% of the discovered world but the Dangelhosens and their contacts were saying exciting things about the Russian Empire and Conisbrough was keen to find out. The Crimean War had ended and slavery (or serfdom) had been abolished for the tens of millions caught in such servitude in that vast expanse; the new leaders looked keen to move on.

The visit wasn't a resounding success but had opened the eyes of many who undertook the journey to the sheer magnificence of the architecture and the ambitious and exuberant leadership of the Tsar who Dangelhosen and Conisbrough were privileged to meet at a dinner in honour of a number of businessmen who had been trading with Russia. Aside from a couple of small but groundbreaking treacle contracts in exchange for a regular supply of iron ore little was achieved. That didn't stop the Member for Sheffield standing up in the House of Commons accusing English businessmen of selling out to savages, treason and espionage. The Speaker of the House told him to sit down before he fell down as it appeared he might have exceeded his daily allowance of port, so painfully was his gout affecting him.

Now quite the intrepid traveller Lord Conisbrough, again with Dangelhosen in attendance, spent six months visiting China and Japan the following year. Advice from the Foreign Office had been not to go. Doubtless our Right Honourable friend the member for Sheffield would have had something to say on the subject had he not been hospitalised and was confined to bed with his swollen ankles in bandages. Those countries had been at war with one another but an uneasy peace seemed to be holding. Now seemed as good a time as any.

Following Charles Darwin Conisbrough's lead many members of the dynasty family engaged in research and medical research in particular. While the Conisbroughs had been at the forefront of disease protection and prevention since the outbreak of the Black Death in Sprot in the Middle Ages, rapid advances were being made in medicine across the country and the population increased rapidly with improving life expectancy. But as Professor Acton Yard had demonstrated much of the modern medicine was quackery and medicines did not do what it said on their tin – though they did make small fortunes for the manufacturers (according to Lanbourne who let slip in the Butt Hole one night that he had a few shares). At Charles Darwin's suggestion an understanding of Chinese medicine was placed high on the priority task list.

The rapid increase in the population of Britain opened other doors. The Conisbroughs invested heavily in the railway system as we will explore shortly recognising that London was now the largest city in the world and its appetite for Conisbrough goods was insatiable. It was fortunate that as England and Europe grew millions of people from this straining population chose to emigrate and many Conisbrough family members had also decided to leave these shores and head to Canada, America and South Africa in search of fresh projects – whether independently or as part of a dynasty-sponsored exercise.

Part Three

Part
Three

The Great
Conisbrough Railway

We're not sure if Lady Gab Gab's actions changed the world but they certainly changed Lord Padraig and his views. Rather romantically one of the first things he did (asking Her Ladyship first, of course) was renew his marriage vows in a small ceremony at the Castle – not at the Abbey – which tended to suggest that the frenzied explosion of religious zealotry pervading Conisbrough newspapers was at an end, whatever Beaverbrook might decide. For the first time in Conisbrough history the balance sheet showed less income than expenditure as Lord Padraig authorised numerous non-profit making philanthropic ventures such as the establishment of theatres, music halls, auditoria for more serious pursuits, together with a new swathe of social housing projects across dynasty lands but with no rent increases to tenants.

Cranbourne Lanbourne spluttered and protested at the new policy but Lord Padraig was insistent. Not a man to laugh and enjoy a joke in quite the same way as Lady Gertrude even His Lordship chuckled when Gab Gab described Lanbourne as a politically correct, bed wetting vegetarian dolphin botherer. Gertrude didn't speak any foreign languages but it appeared she had total command of her own. Had the horrendous Lanbourne been made aware of Lady Gertrude's remarks without a shadow of a doubt he would have taken strong exception to being described as vegetarian.

As the 19th century progressed and the first part of what we know as the Industrial Revolution drew to a close, heralding in a new and more familiar second "revolution", the Conisbrough dynasty was well placed. To the west, on their lands spanning the Yorkshire Lancashire border great mills had been constructed and a new phase of the textile industry had been born. There and in their mines machines were slowly taking over from manual labour – delivering better, safer and more efficient production methods but with an acute loss of labour at a time when the population working on or associated with dynasty projects was increasing.

Lord Padraig and Lady Gab Gab were acutely aware of this massive change sweeping over them and, with Cranbourne Lanbourne and other experts in the field of construction and structural engineering, looked to initiate a mammoth project that would utilise spare labour and deliver a legacy of which the dynasty could be proud. Utilising the skills and techniques that George Stephenson Conisbrough and Sir Edward Watkin Conisbrough had been perfecting for a number of years the Great Conisbrough Railway was born.

The original intention had been to drive a high speed route from Conisbrough to the outskirts of London serving the dynasty supported university at Willesden but, thankfully, during the planning stage rather less quaint and more serious objectives were set. By buying up significant tracts of land in the preceding decade Lord Padraig found himself as a major shareholder in the recently constructed Manchester Sheffield and Lincolnshire Railway and Edward Watkin Conisbrough was already a Director of that company. Padraig made him Chairman of the Great Conisbrough Railway, the objectives being to develop a quicker way of getting dynasty treacle, coal, iron, steel and textiles to the major growth areas in the south while providing the local people with a faster, more direct and cheaper alternative to the other railway companies that were springing up. The Conisbroughs did not want to join forces with the other companies – despite there being many invitations – as progress seemed to be being measured by the amount of squabbling that occurred in meetings and the millions of pounds being paid out in compensation to landowners.

The main cost seemed to be replacing demolished houses and businesses in the towns and cities on the route so the Conisbrough Board decided to both go in as straight a line as possible but also avoid built up areas and centres of population already well served by other well known companies. It worked. The Conisbroughs had decided not to stop at every lamppost but to make speed the major factor in driving the route. The Great Conisbrough Railway was the success the Board had hoped it would be and opened for business in 1899 just months before the eleventh Lord Padraig left us. Its closure was far swifter and more brutal.

When sold on to the nation in 1948 the value of the line had increased twenty times. In a move that must have had taxpayers either raging in incredulity or with jaws gaping like some sick ruminant the line was closed twenty years later. The Conisbroughs found that decision as perplexing as many that successive governments continue to make whatever their political hue. It seemed to the Board that for every good decision made by those running the rail network, hospitals, police and the schools there are three or four ranging from the poor and incomprehensible to the downright wrong and utterly uncomfortable. Conisbrough decided in the 1960s to turn his back on the nationalised railway and use road transport instead for the dynasty's logistical needs. Padraig invited his cousin Stobart Conisbrough to work out a national logistical plan for all Conisbrough products moving around the country.

Stobart No Bit Part

Stobart was as forward thinking as most Conisbroughs and from his base within the dynasty stronghold of Northamptonshire had a profitable infrastructure and support services operation that he had slowly developed in to a national haulage and logistics company. Lord Padraig, turning his back on the railways the dynasty had once built, owned and nurtured, found the service and reputation of the modern railway quite shocking.

The final straw had come in the late 60s when the dynasty was attempting to deliver freight shipments from Yorkshire to Cornwall. Lanbourne was advised by his contact at British Railways that it would take four days. Desperately trying (and succeeding) to think on his feet Lanbourne had questioned both the astronomical cost and the duration. Apparently it was not profitable for the railway to deliver goods to your chosen destination so, effectively, they took them somewhere close, in this case Plymouth which isn't close at all if you wanted the west of the county as was the case here, and then plonked the goods on trucks for onward despatch by road. Actually plonking seems to suggest quite a quick movement and this certainly wasn't the least bit swift.

At the next Conisbrough Board meeting, to which a senior sales representative from British Railways was invited but failed to attend, a policy of using road haulage for all freight transfer was adopted. This policy remains in place to this day. Through a combination of stupidity (lack of foresight might be a more polite way of saying things) and overcharging for an inferior service the customer was lost. We'd like to say that customers are now heading the other way but, sadly, that would be a fib. Needless to say Stobart's team was able to deliver the shipment, door to door, in sixteen hours at a fraction of the cost and with significantly less risk.

High Speed Train of Thought

The ultimate irony for Padraig Conisbrough came when he was contacted very recently for assistance and preliminary discussions by a senior official with overall project management responsibility for HS2 – the high speed rail line designed to reinvigorate the northern powerhouse. Lord Conisbrough met him at his offices in London. At first the sales pitch had a sensible, honest almost familiar ring to it but the longer it went on it became as stultifyingly boring as one of Lanbourne's anecdotes and it occurred to His Lordship that the raison d'être behind this exciting and worthwhile project was identical to the project aims and objectives that his grandfather had been heavily involved with in the 1870s.

It didn't end there because the official said that one of the routes being considered by ministers for public consultation was the precise route of the long defunct Great Conisbrough Railway. Padraig was usually well prepared and assured during business meetings and, with some justification, believed he had seen and heard it all before. Not on this occasion. The official, Rich Marley, immaculately dressed but a sort of abrasive civil service cocktail of arrogance and Armani, looked equally discombobulated as His Lordship's eyes rolled and, uncharacteristically, Padraig made motions as if attempting to pull out a piece of rogue sausage from between his teeth.

With his wits very much about him, notwithstanding the small whisky Higson had served him at breakfast, Lord Padraig said that he would be a supporter of the project but asked why he was being consulted as all the land and infrastructure had been sold when the line was nationalised. Marley, hair neater than Mary Poppins's underwear drawer, said he didn't believe everything had been sold to HMG. Lanbourne, who had been sitting quietly at the other end of the table pretending to take notes, writing nothing but hearing and seeing everything, asked if he might interject.

Without invitation but correctly assuming he had the floor Lanbourne explained that when the deal had been done with the new British Railways Board in the late 1940s the entire infrastructure had indeed been sold. The land on which the railway was built was also purchased by British Railways but with the codicil that, if not used for railway purposes, the land would revert to Conisbrough ownership on the expiry of a fifty year lease period that would commence once no train service was provided. Marley agreed that was also his understanding but welcomed the confirmation. You could tell Marley didn't, in fact, know this because of the way he managed to pour his double espresso down his trousers and began to ruffle his beautifully waxed and Brylcreemed bouffant.

Beginning to enjoy himself Lanbourne, who had a PhD in Stating the Obvious on occasions, said that provided the high speed line was in operation by 2018 there would be no costs to the project – the former Great Conisbrough Railway having been closed to all traffic in 1968. The moment developers and operators failed to meet the 2018 deadline negotiations would have to commence on a new arrangement. Lanbourne announced that 98.7% of the original track bed was still in place; the other 1.3% had other uses including the Rugby Labour Party Headquarters. Lanbourne and Marley both knew that the project would struggle to find its own nose to pick by 2018 let alone deliver any kind of High Speed Railway.

While Lanbourne might have been impressed with his own knowledge of the figures Marley clearly wasn't and he let slip one of those little high-pitched titters that is supposed to be a hearty laugh but gets caught halfway up the windpipe. Marley wanted the toilet, a taxi back to his offices and a dry cleaner – preferably in that order. As the meeting broke up Lord Padraig asked, perfectly innocently, whose idea it had been all those years ago to revert to a lease if operations ceased. "That would have been your father's, my Lord" said Lanbourne bursting with pride in someone else's achievement for the first time in his life but doubtless wishing that honour had been his firm's.

Lord Conisbrough and Lanbourne left the meeting without uttering another word and went their separate ways. Lanbourne wasn't mistaken when he sensed Padraig Conisbrough had shot him a look of daggers as they walked out. How much Cranbourne Lanbourne had made for the dynasty by selling a small tract of land in the Midlands to the Rugby Labour Party would have to wait for another day.

East Ender Fender Bender

As with all narrow-minded, disagreeable and massively wealthy individuals Cranbourne Lanbourne Ripoff and Scarper were extremely private about their personal lives – even though we only wanted some basic background for this novel – and even more cagey, testy and defensive about their business transactions whether they were on behalf of the Conisbroughs or one of their other private clients. You could read plenty of nothingness about their activity in the press, online and in their numerous pompous publications but in all the column inches there wasn't a single word about the men themselves or any detailed analysis of the work. Attempting to gain access to their magnificent offices near Holborn Viaduct was futile – this after numerous requests for an appointment had been curtly declined by the abrupt but supremely well-trained support team. A team of bodybuilders, steroid manufacturers and the headquarters of the secret service of a small but wealthy African dictatorship seemed to occupy the lobby of their building and, valuing the integrity of our limbs, we beat a very hasty retreat indeed.

Such a level of privacy and protection surrounding Cranbourne Lanbourne Ripoff and Scarper suggested that the firm didn't want anyone to know anything about them or their activities whatsoever. The squads of bruisers in Holborn Viaduct was perfectly normal for a firm of this high a profile, we told ourselves. We couldn't envision those Cranbourne Lanbourne employees doing anything illegal in the 21st century world of business, for example.

Undeterred and after several pints of Dutch courage (sadly not a Neumann brew) we decided to follow whoever emerged from the beautiful Victorian building first. It didn't prove easy as one of the aforementioned bodybuilders brought a black SUV with tinted windows to the front of the building and loaded a substantial puffed-up cargo in a hand tailored Christian Dior suit quicker than we could hail a cab. Follow that bodybuilder didn't go down well as an instruction with Terry, the cabbie unlucky enough to stop for us but we were soon drifting east skirting the City of London and roaring through Blackfriars – wondering whether the driver of the SUV ahead had learned his traffic skills in Calcutta, Manila or on Streatham Ice rink.

In Terry Tilling (or Tel, as we gathered he preferred) our bodybuilder had met his match. If you ever want to find out how to drive in the City followed by heading east along the Mile End Road and Bow Road just ask Tel. Which was our mistake on any one of a number of levels because, having asked, Tel was obliged to answer – for the next four hours so it turned out. As we had proceeded down Commercial Road Tel reeled off how he had, on our behalf (in hot pollute, was the phrase he used) committed twenty driving offences in the space of sixty seconds. We could guess at two or three: speeding, jumping a red light and endangering the life of a Police Community Support Officer were bankers but we'd obviously had our eyes closed when he performed these additional manoeuvres and functions:-

Mounting the kerb and endangering pedestrians

Overtaking a bus which has indicated to pull out (seven times, Your Honour)

Colliding with a cyclist and failing to stop

Driving with no hands on the wheel

Excessive use of the horn

Ramming a parked car

Use of bus only – no taxis – lane

Rude and obscene gestures to a police motorcyclist

Driving without looking in the direction of travel

Inappropriate use of a yellow box junction

Endangering oncoming traffic by driving on the wrong side of the road

Travelling the wrong way down a one way street

Driving in a pedestrian only walkway endangering the public

Leaving a traffic light controlled junction before light has turned to green

Shouting and swearing at an elderly pedestrian for "looking at me"

Overuse of full beam headlights blinding other road users

Failing to stop when required to do so by a Traffic Warden

As Tel prattled on about how the company Bieber (we think he meant rival cab firm Uber) was going to spell the end of taxi services in London we had an inspirational moment. Remembering from far back that Cranbourne Lanbourne Ripoff and Scarper had bought property in Stratford, we wondered if they still had a house there and that would prove our destination. We warned Tel but there was no need as he knew Stratford like the back of his hand. Not that the backs of his hands were available as he seemed to have mastered the skill of manoeuvring his cab while having his hands in the front pocket of his West Ham United hoodie.

Amazed that we had kept in touch with our prey on the thirty minute/£100 journey the SUV made an abrupt stop near Bow Quarter and then disappeared into an underground car park beneath what appeared to be a five storey block of apartments. Actually "block" is not a fair description as the building was more like a boutique hotel from our vantage point with mature trees obscuring the A12 and well tended planted gardens at the front. Needing desperately to heed the call of nature we left the cab and asked Tel to wait. "You pay; I stay" was the well rehearsed but cheerful response.

Having completed our priority business and having a snoop around our hearts sank when we saw the brother of one of the bodybuilders at the front desk of the building. It appeared that there were four apartments (presumably one each for the partners) on the four upper floors and the ground floor was devoted to recreation, relaxation and, of course, protection. The bodybuilder brother looked worse the closer we got; like someone had punched him in the face for several hours without stopping and then the wounds had been left to heal without treatment. The access to the parking garage had long since smashed shut with the sound of metal on concrete. There was nothing for it but to go to the door.

There followed one of those pointless conversations that only the Two Ronnies have been able to master. We go up to the front door and notice that the bodybuilder has a hook where his left hand should have been. Even though it had only been two minutes suddenly we needed the toilet again. "Ripoff?" "Scarper" came the reply. We never did find out if he wanted us to leave or had misheard our request. "Howza hook?" "He lives next door at number 73". So it went on as communicating through three inch armour plated glass wasn't ideal and the intercom appeared to have been switched off. It didn't look promising so we decided to retreat to the peace and tranquillity of Tel's cab where, like one of those old and short-lived 8-track car stereo players on a reel, our driver was on the second playing of when David Cameron and Helena Bonham-Carter had used his cab and blah blah you'll never guess whose underwear I found rabbit rabbit.

One story he told that we found amusing was when he was driving past a house in Shenfield with a sign out front saying 'Talking Dog For Sale'. "I stopped and rang the bell and the dog's owner says to go round to the back garden", explained Tel. "I saw a nice old Labrador Retriever sitting there so said do you really talk?" "Yes," the Labrador replied. "After recovering from the shock of hearing the dog talk I asked him to tell me his story".

The Labrador looked up and said, "Well, I discovered that I could talk when I was pretty young. I wanted to help the government, so I was sold to MI6. In no time at all they had me jetting from country to country, sitting in rooms with spies and world leaders; because no one imagined that a dog would be eavesdropping I was one of their most valuable spies for eight years. But the jetting around really tired me out and I knew I wasn't getting any younger so I decided to settle down. I signed up for a job at Gatwick Airport to do some undercover security work, wandering near suspicious characters and listening in. I uncovered some incredible dealings and was awarded several medals. Then I got married, had a few puppies, and now I've just retired."

"I was absolutely gobsmacked so I went back into the house and asked the owner how much he wants for the dog." "Ten quid," the owner said. "£10! But your dog is absolutely amazing! Why on earth are you selling him so cheaply?" "Because he's a lying bastard... he's never been further than Southend."

Tel Tells a Tale

Waiting seemed a good idea and, sure enough, an hour or so later a BMW estate emerged from its subterranean fortress. Invited to follow, Tel took us a few miles back along the route we'd travelled to Canary Wharf where the driver of the BMW (a cross between a Tarantino Samuel L Jackson and Mike Tyson) deposited Lanbourne and the shadowy figure of Ripoff at a high end and exclusive restaurant. Bunging the Maitre D a large tip we were able to ascertain that the table for four had been booked under the name of Shackell. Throwing another £20 note on his pulpit he allowed access to the inner sanctum where, not wishing to be recognised for fear of damage to our professional reputation as serious writers, we quickly identified the greasy Lanbourne, a sneaky Ripoff and what looked like identical twin sisters in beautiful and very expensive cocktail dresses.

We were unlikely to get anywhere that evening with Lanbourne and Ripoff ensconced with lady friends for the duration. Recalling the fine wines seen on display near the Maitre D one might imagine Lanbourne would be taking his time. Inviting Tel to return us to Canary Wharf Docklands station and on paying him his £350 plus a tip he asked us, out of the blue, what we had been up to and we told him. Tel wanted to know why we hadn't just asked him in the first place instead of wasting time and spending a load of money needlessly. Probably because we hadn't been able to get a word in edgeways. Slightly bemused he explained that every taxi driver out east knows "the crowd at Bow Quarter" and he could give us chapter and verse on the "comings and goings at that building". Running short of £20 notes we declined but took Tel's mobile number for the next instalment of this family history. Alternatively we might just ask him to record a voice message for us.

Two Little Boys had Two Little Toys

The present day Wilson Nettleham and Richard Holton have always been firm friends and attended Lincoln Academy for Young Gentlemen (which has these days been converted in to a Young Offenders Institution run by Group 4). Like the myopic Ayrton Speckmeister many years earlier, both were bullied to within an inch of total humiliation by their fellow pupils. Holton, whose face was used by his art teacher as the mould for a monster mask much to the class's amusement, was nicknamed the Devil's Reject by his peers for, when doing his hair each morning, his mother would gel up two little clumps which could be mistaken for horns.

Wilson Nettleham was an academic genius and, aside from his sibling-like relationship with Holton, a complete loner. Fluent in Latin, French, German, Ancient Greek and Russian by the age of 15 it was rumoured that the Foreign Office had their eye on him for one of their special departments, which said as much about the F&CO as it did about their potential recruit. His other passion was modelling whether it be in wood or plastic but his tyrannical father, tiring and jealous of his son showing much more promise than he ever had, took obvious pleasure in destroying the wondrous bus, aircraft and locomotive models that Wilson would bring home. It was rumoured that Wilson Senior was fond of the odd model himself but not the type that would leave glue and balsa wood shavings on the bed sheets.

Before he had reached senior school age his father had refused Wilson permission to walk the short distance to watch the trains passing through the cutting in the village because the railway company was part owned by the Conisbroughs. The young man watched the traffic instead, not that there was much, perhaps dreaming of an escape from the prison that was Nettleham. Wilson formed a relationship with the local bus drivers and soon learned that when they put two fingers up at him it meant they were two minutes late; one finger, one minute late. He also learned that bus drivers couldn't count beyond two. Wilson found an ally in Holton, whose model buildings and drawings of dogs earned him invitations to the local craft events where he was frequently awarded seventh and eighth place rosettes. Together they formed a modelling club which, to this day, has only two members.

Any dreams and ambitions Wilson and Holton might have harboured about escaping their dull and depressing lives were shattered by the responsibility both felt to carry on the good work of the Nettleham and Holton families.

Kiss Me Honey,
Honey Kiss Me

Meanwhile back in Sprotbrough conditions had, after nearly one thousand years, gradually begun to improve. To say this had something to do with sprots leaving the area for pastures new would be a cruel but true assessment. The only route west was via Conisbrough and sprot males refused to travel this way fearful of some dreadful but imagined disaster that would strike them. So they went the long way round via Chesterflood in search of a new beginning. The ancestors of one of the original émigrés, Dick Spraysprot, still lived in Mold across the border in modern day Wales and were following in old Dick's footsteps with trouble never far away.

The Mold sprots had taken great pride in being among the first families to be transported to the Americas and Australia for "borrowing" imported tea and other exotic cargos from Liverpool docks in 18th century. Not only had the Spraysprots forgotten to pay for the imported infusions from their suppliers, they had neglected to pay Customs Excise duty or the penalties imposed for such infractions.

In today's Mold Ricardo Spraysprot is the queen bee (or should that be king bee?). Recently this inventive Spraysprot had taken to keeping bees. At first the authorities thought this was some sort of scam (who can blame them?) or a ruse so that Ricardo could go burgling houses wearing his beekeeper's clothing as a disguise and without detection. After the council had had a little think about that one even they rejected the notion as implausible. In fact Ricardo Spraysprot was genuinely keeping bees as a tax deductable business venture. Doubtless Cranbourne Lanbourne could have advised of better ways but their paths would never cross.

Sensibly the authorities decided to keep Ricardo under surveillance. Nonsensically they appointed a local sprot constable to the duty. PC Plodsprot was a local man and had known Ricardo since their schooldays together. In fact Plodsprot knew everybody in Mold as it was a small community with the sheep population outnumbering the humans. The town had nothing to recommend it. The Wetherspoons, once the focal point of the town centre along with the Job Seekers Office, had closed due to fire damage and there was no plan to reopen the premises. In truth the Wetherspoons closed every Sunday for repairs after the excesses of the steroid-driven customers on Saturday nights. Reopening the following Friday the same ritual would be performed. Failing to take in the requisite profits from the lucrative steak night as it was always closed (and due to the insurers pulling the plug) it shut up shop.

Ricardo situated his bee hives in a small field in the caravan he had made his home when the local branch of scientologists threw him out. Remarkably the sheep in the field tolerated the bees – more than likely because they were the only species that hadn't tried to molest them at every opportunity. The caravan was on the edge of town near Dick's meadow, so named because the legendary Dick Spraysprot was rumoured to use it as his toilet. These days the noxious miasma had abated somewhat and didn't seem to bother the bees who gobbled up the nectar from the wild flowers that grew in thick clumps around Ricardo's caravan and the edge of the meadow.

We don't know whether Ricardo knew this straightaway or not as he is silent on the matter and we have been unable to access his prison records but there was something odd about the flowers in the meadow. It would seem, by logical deduction, that Dick Spraysprot had planted opium poppies all those years ago and had enjoyed the harvest (we doubt whether it was for the relief of his lumbago). We suspect Ricardo Spraysprot noticed the magical properties of the honey collected from his hives when queues of Scousers appeared at the door of his caravan every Thursday after cashing their benefit cheques.

The sophisticated drug users just across the Mersey River had long since been looking for a buzz to spread on their toast when they got up in the afternoon and Spraysprot's honey filled this void. The purity of the honey was staggering and the business venture would have gone on considerably longer for Ricardo had the Accident and Emergency department of the Liver Hospital not noticed a trend of spaced out scallywags being admitted most days in the early afternoon requiring the stomach pump and evacuation of various orifices due to opium overload.

PC Plodsprot was on the case and, armed with the

intelligence from Liver Hospital that a drug supplier was active in the area, set about developing a strategy to capture the Big Cheese working on his patch. After a few days he rejected his idea of going undercover in plain clothes because, while he knew everyone in Mold, everyone in the whole county either knew or had seen newspaper cartoons of Plodsprot by virtue of his reputation as a terrier-like crime fighter.

Days of Fines and Closures

Within the space of two years PC Plodsprot had come close to cracking the case – albeit by accident. As a lover of treacle and sweet things our intrepid guardian of law and order had been able to purchase a jar of Ricardo's honey when his most recent expenses claim had been settled. Spreading the delightful gooey contents on his buttered crumpet he settled down in front of the TV to watch Hollyhocks with a can of Watbread's finest electric soup. Plodsprot soon felt simultaneously enthused by the normally dull and uninspiring soap opera while enduring the most agonising pains in his stomach and was rushed to the Liver Hospital by a neighbour alarmed at his antics in her garden with his can of drink and her undergarments off the wash line.

Whether the hospital or Plodsprot deserves the credit for bringing the case to its conclusion is up to you to decide but predictably Ricardo's honey was singled out by local health officials as the cause of the longstanding pandemic. Ricardo, brought before the local magistrates, laughed and giggled like a hyena that had consumed his product when the case against him was dismissed. The Chair of the Mold Magistrates directed that Ricardo had no control over what his bees gathered. Consequently he could not be held responsible for the five and half million pounds spent on tackling the problem in the area, the astronomical policing bill nor the six hundred and fifty new addicts on the Liver drug users register. Ricardo gave double thumbs up to the public gallery.

Public Health officials and the Tax Office disagreed with Ricardo's claim of innocence. Sadly deportation to Australia was no longer a punishment available to the Crown Court in Chester who promptly packed Ricardo Spraysprot off to Wrexham prison where he joined the vast majority of the population of Mold. PC Plodsprot was promoted to Sergeant and secured a lucrative all expenses paid posting to Romford in Essex where he was placed in charge of the drug squad. We must point out that, taking his cue from the jailbird Ricardo, there is no substantiated evidence that Plodsprot is involved in the manufacture and distribution of so called "legal highs" in the county.

It was only right that we contacted Plodsprot about the disciplinary case against him following the discovery of a cocktail of drugs in his locker. He claimed variously that these were samples and he held them for "operational reasons". We're glad at least that he listened during his sergeants' training course. When challenged on the noticeable buzzing sound in his office Plodsprot claimed this was just the Chief Superintendent's hearing aid.

Let's Settle Them in Nettleham

These days Nettleham and, to a lesser extent, the surrounding area managed by Sir Richard of Holton, is not only a shadow of its former self but a complete sunset. The once beautiful village has been transformed by the building of the "Lincolnshire Open Prison and Sprot Rehabilitation Camp" on its outskirts where once prize winning hops had been grown by previous Nettleham generations. All the way from the bus stop by the village green down the main street to the camp there was litter, faeces, broken bottles, syringes, condoms and knuckle dusters. Yes, you've guessed it, the centre was run by Group 4 and their care in recruiting staff had been as meticulous as ever.

Baron Wilson von Nettleham, as the present day incumbent of the title continues to like to be known, inherited a right royal mess from earlier generations and despite suffering from never having done a day's work in his life was coping remarkably well despite his difficult childhood. Wilson congratulated himself that, unlike many people, his family had "seen off" the inexorable advance of the Conisbroughs. The fact that property developers, scammers, local authorities and most villagers had "seen him coming" was neither here nor there.

In order to pay his way Nettleham land had had to be sold, or practically given away, to developers and house builders who have ripped the heart and soul out of Nettleham Village with their sensitive and careful plans for the environment. The brook which never flooded in a thousand years was placed in an ugly culvert so additional profits could be made by building a Dominos Pizza delivery outlet atop it. The water supply dried up, the ducks went to a Chinese restaurant in Lincoln and the lake became a skate park. Baron Nettleham has retained numerous properties for the benefit of any future generations, a filling station and motor repair shop and the finest model railway store in the area.

Sir Richard of Holton has fared little better and much of the Holton lands have had to be sold with Holton retained by the new owners to manage the area, including cutting the grass at the race course.

Celebration of the Excavation

After vacating the exhausted treacle mine and oil well at Welton in Lincolnshire the Conisbroughs were keen to maintain a foothold in the area if only for the large number of local employees loosely managed by Ayrton Speckmeister, heir to the myopic Speckmeister we met centuries earlier, from his home in the East Midlands. You will recall that the Conisbroughs bestowed a house near Chesterflood to the Speckmeisters in perpetuity. Unfortunately the Ayrton Speckmeister of that period had not married wisely and his wife Avengia took in sprot lodgers to satisfy her increasingly lavish lifestyle and numerous other urges. One Bonfire Night, experimenting with explosives stolen, no doubt, from a Conisbrough mining operation, one of the lodgers, now known locally as the Gunpowder Sprot, not only blew himself up but destroyed Ayrton's home and badly damaged a local church. Passing through Chesterflood today you can still see how the massive explosion caused the church spire to bend.

While Ayrton returned to his mother's home with the children, Avengia, no doubt made miserable by the destruction of her designer clothing collections and her pustule infested lover, disappeared with a sprot travelling salesman and never returned, even when the house was rebuilt. It was rumoured at the time that she was seen heading south on the back of a mule with a sprot wearing nothing but socks, sandals and a smile (the sprot, not Avengia who was always immaculately turned out).

But we digress. Soil analysis suggested that there was a further rich seam of treacle near the surface in the locality but all planning applications for the necessary fracking exploration were being opposed by our infamous local landowner, Baron Wilson von Nettleham who had what was bordering on paranoia about decisions made by the Planning Committee and became apoplectic when the Conisbroughs were mentioned. Now the Conisbroughs had traditionally managed opposition and situations like this through negotiation and settlement and this was no different. Lord Padraig suggested to Nettleham that he stop his silliness or he would open a rival model railway shop in Lincoln driving trade away from the Nettleham outlet. Nettleham could barely contain his tears for the reality (of this threat as he saw it) would spell the end of the period of wealth and independence for him and his family. Reluctantly he agreed to keep quiet when the local planners met. If there was one thing that would make Wilson turn against his friend and neighbour it would be his unnatural devotion to his beloved model shop.

At the Planning Committee meeting Nettleham's silence on the matter was a source of sadness to Sir Richard of Holton, who still owned properties in Market Rasen and had management control of the railway between Nettleham and Wrawby through his day job with Network Rail. A dull and unintelligent man, to this day he is unaware how his treacle was taken from him. Conisbrough obtained the necessary compulsory purchase order to allow treacle to be mined underneath his now defunct signalbox at Holton-le-Moor. Foolishly Sir Richard never expected Conisbrough to act and left his trusty hound, Captain Charles Humber, the black Labrador, on guard in the deserted signal box on the eve of the excavation. Sensing another advantage over his rival Conisbrough took the hound prisoner as he was on his property.

After many years as a lookout for Network Rail on this stretch of line Captain Charles is now employed by the dynasty as a bouncer at the Chesterflood Wetherspoons. Word has it the Captain has never been happier. The Chesterflood outlet is frequented by more than the odd sprot and he delights in nibbling and aggravating the pustules on their buttocks when they step out of line (which, to be fair, is most of the time). His fellow bouncers, while colossal brainless pricks, report tales of Holton mistreating the Captain by leaving him out in all weathers without the appropriate workwear.

Sir Richard has yet to come to grips with the loss of his signalbox and his hound. Many have suggested that he was more devastated at losing Captain Charles than his assets and have hinted that his relationship with Labradors was unhealthy and there was more to it than met the eye. Sir Richard still refuses to engage with the Conisbroughs and one senses that the snivelling pair of Nettleham and Holton would plot revenge against Padraig – if they weren't too naive to think of a way.

They think it's all over - it is now!

But what of the man behind the mask? We'd discovered so little about the real Lord Padraigs and their personal relationships with Her Ladyship down the years that we felt we were missing out on whole chunks of interesting history that the reader deserves to access. To this end we managed to persuade Lord Padraig to share a few entries from his personal diary and, randomly, we chose 1966 the year after he assumed the title of Lord Padraig Conisbrough. You will recall that Padraig and Lady Wendy Geek Geek were already married and had two children.

Lord Padraig wrote:-

Friday 29th July 1966

My tan is fading. We've only been back from Aberdovey less than a day. Stayed at a hotel on the seafront there straight out of the Norman Bates Psycho chain. Lady Geek Geek has contracted several viruses. Children waking at 0300hrs this morning complaining of jet lag. It was only Wales but they've convinced themselves we were abroad and won't go back to sleep. Telling the mother-in-law about the holiday was a mistake as she thought I said Abu Dhabi not Aberdovey and was worried Lady Wendy had caught dysentery, pleurisy, hypocrisy or lunacy; she kept on going on about camels, the Islamic State, sand and OPEC and I'm sure she still hasn't grasped it.

Geek Geek now has full-blown lie-in-bed-moaning flu. I am sure it is terrible but what about me. She is only on the brink of death, Higson and the servants are still on holiday and I have two jet-lagged monsters to contend with. And what about the three suitcases of dirty laundry Wendy has asked to me to sort out, there's no food in the kitchen and I've a pile of mail in my study to deal with. Geek Geek won't tolerate Lanbourne in the house so it'll just have to wait. The first thing I need to do is complete a three year residential PhD on how this new thing called a washing machine works. Why can't it wait for the bloody servants?

Whose (word omitted) idea was it to get into electrical goods anyway? If men did the majority of washing in the nation's homes they wouldn't be allowed to be designed by (word omitted as not sure all readers are over 18). What on earth is wrong with ON and OFF instead there's a choice of programme. What! Is it a bloody television as well? Does it show (word omitted) cartoons? And how do you open the door when it's finished whizzing around?

Meanwhile I am being shot at by a psychotic dwarf dressed as a (Native American – ed) with an authentic six shooter probably stolen from the lifeless body of some cavalryman (his sister). I haven't eaten for two days now and there's just time for a quick sprint up several flights of stairs with a honey and lemon vick aspirin gin cocktail and utter to Wendy in my best sickly voice "Are you feeling any better, Darling?" All Wendy can say from her death bed in between throwing up and going into convulsions is, "I'm sorry, Padraig". Sorry? Sorry? She bloody well will be sorry when I put her out of her misery and suffocate her under her duck feather-filled pillow. Nothing inhumane about voluntary euthanasia you know.

30ᵀᴴ July 1966

Just as the hell on earth is relenting and Wendy has transferred her misery to the large sofa in the living room (just a tiny piece of toast with honey would be lovely, please Darling etc.) I notice that the World Cup Final between England and West Germany is about to start. (Word omitted) jammy Dangelhosen (word omitted) has got tickets. At least I have the only colour television set in the country thanks to the boffins at Conisbrough Electricals. All thoughts of family health, domestic duties or dealing with administration are put to one side for this serious priority,

Having piled Wendy up with a mountain of pillows, blankets, drugs and remedies Psycho Dwarf wakes from his nap. "Father, I've got a head/nose/ear/tummy/arm/brain ache". I eye the authentic six shooter on his night stand with envy and appalling thoughts just as the first goal of the game is being described downstairs. "Something happened in your game" says Geek Geek helpfully from her grandstand seat on the sofa.

After finally soothing the little chap back to sleep with the help of his Higson hand puppet I sprint downstairs only to forget the low beam on the landing. Tumbling down the rest of the stairs I am writhing in agony on the hallway floor when Kenneth Wolstenholme describes England's equalising goal as "unmissable". Well it might have been "unmissable" for Martin Peters or Geoff Hurst (I didn't see it so I can't say) but the whole (word omitted) experience is proving rather too elusive for me.

As I sat down rubbing my head the whistle is blown for half time. "Is that it over now? Shall we watch something else?" enquires Her Ladyship who is blissfully unaware how close she has come to being thrown off the balcony along with her (word omitted) flowering peonies and trailing ivy. At least, as the cameraman pans in on Dieter Dangelhosen with a huge sausage and a pint of beer, someone is enjoying himself.

As the second half commences the telephone rings. It's Wendy's mother. She's been having some trouble with her leg to the extent that she's started talking about it in the third person as if it were no longer attached to her body. The leg didn't want to get out of the car this morning; the leg was seen by the doctor after he'd surgically replaced my brain etc. There's a scream from the sitting room as England score. "The England team have won, Darling" shouts Lady (word omitted) just loud enough to prompt a full arsenal of questions about her health and recovery. The conversation goes on and on regurgitating the confusion from the previous day about Abu Dhabi. There is a groan which likely signals a West German equaliser. I reciprocate and that error of judgement and revelation of my human side gives my mother-in-law the opportunity to give one of the most acclaimed and powerful men in Britain a good old-fashioned lecture.

Coming off the telephone and heading back to join Lady Geek Geek in the living room it starts ringing again. "Where are you?" enquires our daughter who had been at the shops with friends. "You were supposed to collect me five minutes ago. There are no taxis – there must be something special happening". Tell me about it. Rushing I crash the car into some of Lady Geek Geek's favourite garden gnomes on the way up the drive. It helps to have hands on the wheel. I enter the sitting room to see Nobby Stiles dancing with the World Cup and Lady Wendy holding out her tea cup.

The Transformation of the Transportation

You've probably been wondering how the Conisbroughs came to be running the railways in London. You're not the only ones. It is a sordid and distasteful tale – as grim and despicable as the Bully of Harlesden who was in charge of operations on behalf of the dynasty in those days. It started many generations earlier when Isambard Kingdom Conisbrough, a renowned, skilled and sought after engineer, built a suspension bridge over the River Con thus ending the physical separation between Conisbrough and Sprot. To this day no sprot male has dared cross the bridge fearing a trap similar to the one their forefathers suffered over 900 years earlier. Sprot women trot over quite happily to buy and sell in Conisbrough market and just to get away from the bepustuled, carbuncle ridden males of the species.

Such was the magnificence of this bridge, a truly masterful feat never attempted before, that Isambard was asked to design and mastermind a number of projects, many of them rail related and many in London. One such project, a tunnel under the Thames was mesmerising in its sheer brilliance. Ever the shrewd Conisbrough, Isambard negotiated a small royalty on every person and vehicle using the tunnel. The owners, at the time the Liberal Democrat-run council agreed, never thinking that the tunnel would prove so popular. Within months the leader of the council, Ken Levenshulme, sought to renegotiate, offering Conisbrough control over what we nowadays know as London Overground in exchange for his lifetime royalty entitlement. Rather strangely after consulting the family, Isambard agreed. The railways were a loss making mess so Levenshulme assumed Conisbrough would never exercise his option. Levenshulme was right; but the option remained exercisable by the dynasty indefinitely.

Overground was run by a horrendous man who, in his early years in charge of locomotive and maintenance depots, used to run round the engine sheds raising his bowler hat and shrieking "You're fired!" Alan Sugar-style at any poor apprentice who didn't cut the mustard. The security guard on the gate was the busiest man there with a constant stream of apprentices leaving in tears or arriving in expectation. The Bully of Harlesden was a sharp and intelligent man having graduated from the University of Willesden with honours and a degree in People Skills and Personal Hygiene and was mightily proud of his achievements. Bully had but one weakness in that he was besotted with his personal assistant, a not unattractive sprot girl from Swiss Cottage renowned for her party tricks with a bottle of Merlot whether full or empty. Her best performance was reserved for a Christmas awards party (totally rigged in her favour by the Bully naturally). On being announced to the stage to receive her award Shazza Hotbox (who had been drinking all afternoon with the driver of the company train) took a gulp of Merlot and popped an

Alka Seltzer in her mouth at the same time. Her acceptance speech consisted of her proclaiming she was possessed by the Devil as the fizzing and spurting pinkish red mixture spilled from her mouth. Quite a girl our Shazza. The Hotbox family was making quite an impression on 21st century London.

The present day Lord Conisbrough had yet to exercise his option, gained many years earlier by his ancestor, but one evening while travelling on the tube with the toady Lanbourne of Cranbourne Lanbourne Ripoff and Scarper he encountered the Bully of Harlesden laden down with toys, bought not at Hamleys but at some seedy store in Soho. One particular parcel, the Mouse Muncher, caught Conisbrough's eye for he had seen the same device in Lady Geek Geek's dressing room at Conisbrough Castle. On this occasion the parcel was taking up a seat alongside the obviously inebriated Bully who hurled abuse at anyone attempting to sit down, shrieking "Don't you know who I am? I run the bloody railway so go away". With that he would take another gulp from his carefully concealed flask of Tanquaray. Although off-duty, his baseball cap worn backwards as the ultimate badge of imbecility, the Bully was a public official seemingly abusing his position.

Disgusted with the Bully's behaviour Lord Padraig instructed Lanbourne to make enquiries of Harlesden and his boasts, draw up papers for the exercise of the Conisbrough option and ensure the horrendous Bully was kicked as far away from the railway as a hobnail boot could deliver him. Cranbourne Lanbourne are as despicable and awful as the Bully of Harlesden. That made them some the finest lawyers and accountants in the land and, you will doubtless recall, they had been appointed to serve the dynasty for generations. Some may call it nit picking; others may describe it as attention to detail. Lanbourne soon knew more about the Overground operation than any man alive; and also knew more about the Bully of Harlesden and his autocratic empire than he did himself. The bad news for Lord Conisbrough was that Harlesden had a contract with Overground so watertight that even the devilish Lanbourne could see no way to remove this Bully from his position of power.

The good news from the sneaky Lanbourne was that his firm's enquiries had uncovered the seedy and inappropriate liaison between the Bully and the Merlot swilling Hotbox. Lanbourne put forward a set of proposals to his Lordship that had him purring noisier than at his first encounter with Lady Geek Geek.

At the subsequent meeting between Harlesden, his board of directors and the Conisbrough side the Bully looked positively ashen. This had not been caused by an excess dose of Tanquaray but through a lack of sleep worrying about a future without the delectable Shazza Hotbox. Lanbourne, in a routine meeting with Overground lawyers had proposed job cuts and swingeing reductions in the salaries and pension contributions that the filthy greedy Overground staff had enjoyed for many a year. It just so happened that the Hotbox contract was up for renewal and Lanbourne proposed this should not be renewed as the Bully had no need of four secretaries, his own private train with driver and a personal assistant. The Overground lawyers privately agreed but negotiated the sacrifice of Hotbox in exchange for a tapering of salaries, rather than the cuts proposed by their new governing authority.

Predictably the Bully was incensed, worried, shocked and bewildered when faced with the recommendations from the Overground lawyers. They went round in ever decreasing circles until the Bully was spinning with confusion. Ultimately he agreed to sacrifice his own contract for the renewal of Shazza's and tapering of the obscene salaries paid to his staff. He went without sleep until the meeting with Conisbrough at which he hoped the Overground proposals would be accepted.

At the meeting Lord Conisbrough and Lanbourne agreed the proposals on four conditions. First, the Bully's private train should be made accessible to any Board member or their legal team in connection with their duties; secondly, the Bully's salary would be cut in half; thirdly, he would report directly to His Lordship via Lanbourne; and finally, drug and alcohol testing would be introduced in all operational areas. Shazza Hotbox would live to fight another day. Of all the conditions agreed for reasons unknown the Bully started to shake uncontrollably at the thought of drug testing.

The Overground moved in to a new era following these changes. Profits were reinvested instead of lining the pockets of train drivers, cash flow improved due to better accounting with Lanbourne's beady eyes on the ledger and service reliability improved 10%. The relationship between His Lordship and Harlesden would be a story for another time as will the stories and escapades surrounding the eponymous Hotbox.

The Revelation of
the Impregnation

The Lambournes of Andover had been landowners in Hampshire since the English Civil War when they stood up against Oliver Crimewave during the brutal anti-royalist battles. Lands and titles were bestowed on Sir Percy Lambourne by a grateful monarch on the restoration of the monarchy. The dynasty was a neighbour of Lambourne having a few worked out treacle mines to the north.

The present day Lambourne, Lord Niall, contacted Conisbrough to enquire whether he was interested in selling or leasing (any of) the land as Lambourne had a plan to use the rich soil and gentle slopes for a new wine growing venture.

The dynasty rarely disposed of assets or allowed tenants but Niall Lambourne had been helpful to the dynasty when it had wanted to build a railway connection to the mines linking with Andover's own line through his property. Lord Conisbrough agreed in principle that an arrangement was possible and helpfully waived any rent until the vineyards produced a profit. Conisbrough instructed Cranbourne Lanbourne to prepare the contracts and agreement for heads of terms. One condition was stipulated to Lanbourne and that was that Lord Niall should be able to demonstrate some expertise with wine and wine growing.

Conisbrough arranged for Lanbourne to use the Overground company train for the visit. Unfortunately he would not be accompanied by the Bully of Harlesden who had failed the drug and alcohol test for the 179th consecutive day. In an ironic twist the security guard who had been kept busy years earlier signing out and signing in apprentices terrorised by the Bully was now fully employed writing toxology reports on Harlesden and dozens of his feckless staff. Unbeknown to Harlesden the guard, Luke Owen, a warm and friendly man, had been incentivised by Cranbourne Lanbourne and the dynasty and received a bonus for every report he wrote following a positive test. Luke Owen was consequently the highest paid member of staff receiving a salary marginally more than Harlesden and Hotbox.

As Harlesden's deputy it fell to Shazza Hotbox to accompany Lanbourne on the day. Hotbox had remarkably and surprisingly passed all her drug and alcohol tests since their introduction. Many suspected that the slippery Hotbox was cheating the system by carrying clean samples in her handbag but Luke Owen had insisted that he and his team of nurses had witnessed Shazza passing (no pun intended) with flying colours. As an honest and straightforward man nobody doubted Owen's word as it would be in his interests to fail her.

Lanbourne was bemused by this transformation in Hotbox and was scratching his head all the way from London to Andover as the normally indulgent Shazza ordered coffees from their waitress and failed to spark up her usual joint masquerading as a Dunhill.

On arrival at Andover's private station Lord Niall came aboard with his legal team to go over the paperwork and sign the documentation. Lanbourne then stipulated that he would not sign on behalf of the dynasty until Lord Lambourne had proved his understanding of wine. Lord Niall happily agreed.

The bloated and humourless Lanbourne had brought three or four decent bottles with him (doubtless privately hoping for a session with Hotbox on the return journey) and offered Lord Niall a glass to taste and comment upon.

"It's a Muscat three years old, grown on a north slope, matured in steel containers. Low grade but acceptable."

"That's remarkable," said Lanbourne. "Another glass, please."

"It's a cabernet, eight years old, south-western slope, oak barrels, matured at eight degrees. Requires three more years for finest results."

"Absolutely correct. A third glass."

''It's a pinot blanc champagne, high grade and exclusive," said Lambourne calmly.

Lanbourne was astonished and whispered to Hotbox to suggest something. She left the room and came back in with another glass.

Lambourne tried it.

"It's a bottle blonde, 36 years old, three months pregnant, and if you don't sign the bloody contract I'll name the father."

We don't know which of Lanbourne, Shazza or Lord Niall's lawyer turned the deepest shade of dark puce red. The contracts were hastily and silently agreed and signed, Lord Lambourne departed and the train set off back to London with the task complete but with an awkwardness Lanbourne had not expected an hour earlier. Shazza was wistful and put her headphones on and listened to Siamese Twins by the Cure the whole way; Lanbourne tucked in to the champagne on his own dredging his memory banks for the outcome of the drunken frolic he had enjoyed with Hotbox at the Conisbrough Overground Christmas Party three months earlier. What worried him most was that Hotbox had told him she was 29 years old…

Love Torn Lanbourne

If you were expecting some kind of happy outcome from the cataclysm that was the sordid love triangle of Bully, Shazza and the disgusting Lanbourne you have come to the wrong novel. We suppose Shazza emerges from the debris with some credit. As many of the Hotbox family before her have been able to achieve she was able to turn her life around and ultimately came to work for Lord Padraig in a role she would never have envisaged a year or two earlier.

Shazza had given birth to a healthy baby boy, Axel Hotbox. Although the father's identity was never revealed by Shazza those close to the matter drew their own conclusions. Apparently out of the goodness of their hearts Cranbourne Lanbourne Ripoff and Scarper had donated a substantial lump sum to be held in trust for the boy and a monthly grant for Shazza herself. Doubtless this gesture was designed to purchase Shazza's discretion in the matter. If truth be told Shazza would not have been bursting to reveal any details of the liaison preferring to keep her own council and enjoy her new state of motherhood.

Returning to her office at Overground HQ after her maternity leave some months later Shazza was surprised – and a little amused, we must admit – to find the Bully of Harlesden pushing the refreshment trolley around the Swiss

Cottage complex. It turned out that Bully had been unable to return to operational duties due to his ongoing issues with drink and drugs so it was seen fit to place the once great man in charge of the tea and coffee and where he could be supervised adequately. A broken man, all he had, that hadn't shattered like a bug on the windscreen of one of his trains, was his lifetime contract with Overground.

It wasn't just the devious Lanbourne who thought Shazza and Bully working together in the same environment was a bad idea for Lord Padraig was also monitoring the situation. Impressed by not only Shazza's work ethic but the commendable way in which she had conducted herself since her eyebrow raising and wild days Lord Padraig had her promoted to a new position as Head of Overground Customer Service. Shazza took up the very seat in the very same office occupied by Bully only months earlier, exchanging a wink and a grin with Luke Owen on the security gate as she passed through. There had been no need to worry about customers under the Bully of Harlesden's regime. Almost seven hundred years earlier Shazza's ancestor Henny Hotbox had placed customer service at the top of her agenda.

The ghastly Lanbourne decided to retire (or, probably, it was decided for him by senior partner Cranbourne). The firm couldn't tolerate a whiff of scandal and Lanbourne had increasingly become a bit of a loose cannon. The fact that Cranbourne Lanbourne Ripoff and Scarper had been and would continue to be involved in some of most scandalous and outrageous profit-making and pocket lining ventures seemed irrelevant to their Board. Lanbourne was out.

When we say "out" what we actually mean is Lanbourne's

tenure as partner and Board Member was at an end. His role, for which doubtless he would continue to attract a tear-inducing reward, would be as a non-executive director using Skype to check in to meetings and claim his phenomenal bonus entitlements. Lanbourne, via his ownership of a variety of Channel Island and Cayman Island based property investment companies, would continue to receive an income that would place him in Forbes Magazine – that is, if he were ever willing to reveal his true worth: which is slightly less likely than Hell freezing over. Even less likely than that would be for him to tell Her Majesty's Revenue and Customs his rental income from the apartment in Bow Quarter for which a lease had been drawn up favouring two young female German metallurgy students.

Readers might be thinking Lanbourne lacked a sense of humour. On one of his last evenings in Bow he might have proved us wrong. Accompanied at a discreet distance by one of his "security team" Lanbourne went for a stroll around Bow and Stratford. It wasn't sightseeing. Lanbourne went to each of the eleven ATMs in his area, withdrew £10 on each occasion and left the receipt dangling in the drawer. The next customer at each machine could be forgiven for thinking that Donald Trump was the previous user of the banking service such was the ridiculous figure on Lanbourne's credit balance.

Every Little Helps

We should point out that we did not write the anonymous detailed e-mail to Cranbourne based on our research. In truth it wasn't a moment too soon as Lanbourne, who'd been having trouble with his weight and was growing increasingly self-conscious about his appearance, had been causing a bit of a stir in the local community.

Turning up at his local Tesco Click and Collect and loading his BMW estate car with the help of the staff the purchase of a large sack of dog food was the catalyst for a conversation. When asked what type of dog he had Lanbourne replied that the dog biscuits were for him as he was starting the "Dog Diet" again. Intrigued the young employee asked what this involved. The sarcastic and superior Lanbourne said it was very effective if you load your pockets with the nuggets and take one or two when hungry. The danger was misusing the product as on a previous occasion he had ended up in the local hospital's ICU. Horrified the young employee enquired if the dog food had poisoned him. Lanbourne said this was not the case as he had merely attempted to cross the road to socialise with an Irish Setter when he had been struck by a car. Affronted by the spiteful, sneering Lanbourne the manager was summoned and promptly banned the chubby lawyer from visiting the store – and wrote to Cranbourne about his unpleasant conduct.

The disgraced and disgraceful Lanbourne retired to his villa in Barbados where he proceeded to drink the island dry of rum while being cared for by a sprot houseboy called Croxford. Lanbourne's career had been distinguished, wrote the Financial Times, when news of his retirement filtered out. It is true Lanbourne and the firm had been loyal to the Conisbroughs but had taken their fair share and a bit more besides. Lanbourne's final act as a Board member had been a successful one as a rival firm of accountants run by a group of Sikhs had been ordered by the High Court to pay damages in the seven figures to Cranbourne Lanbourne for using the latter's image on their own advertising beneath the strap line "You tried working with the cowboys now see what the Indians can offer".

If there was one shred of decency in Lanbourne's body it most definitely wasn't near the surface but some months later (as part of ongoing work by the Serious Fraud Office) it would be revealed that the deeds of the villa and lands in Barbados were in Axel Hotbox's name. Whether Axel would go on to play a role in Cranbourne Lanbourne we daren't say for fear of spoiling the next instalment. We can say that Lanbourne, increasingly grumpy and immobile due to his massive weight gain, slowly lost his mind and spent most days muttering, "She said she was 29..." much to Croxford's amusement, while pouring another cuba libre down his distended gullet.

The Bully fared little better. Devastated at how events had conspired against him and, constantly in a Tanquaray and methamphetamine fuelled haze, blaming everyone but himself for his dilemma he finally left Overground. Tired of pushing the refreshment trolley around Swiss Cottage now Hotbox had deserted him he took up a new post with Starburst Mobile Catering and can usually be seen pushing his new trolley, complete with miniature Merlots and the odd tube of electric soup, up and down on the 2200hrs St Pancras to Nottingham, off his face on his own product.

We Are Where We Are. But Where Are We?

The personalities and characteristics of many of the individuals who have made this thousand year adventure so exciting have been examined in some depth. The Cranbourne Lanbourne crowd didn't have any depth to examine but Neumann, Her Ladyship, Higson and others have had our attention at various stages. In the light of this it would only be right to offer a closer and serious look at His Lordship in isolation – what continued to make the head of a remarkable dynasty – that was so much more than a commercial money grabbing organisation – tick. The present day Lord Padraig is the obvious choice as he encapsulates all of the virtues and positivity of previous generations. Or so he says.

Feeling like we were writing his autobiography we pitched up one morning recently at Billericay Conservative Association HQ where Lady Geek Geek had kindly arranged to hire rooms. Fortunately we appeared to have interviewed His Lordship before he had begun to lose his marbles (if that technical medical analysis conforms to the high standards of the rest of this novel). To be honest, and with the benefit of hindsight, it was actually hard to tell if he'd brought all his marbles with him or not. We found him glued to the TV watching reruns of Coronation Street featuring legends like Ena Sharples, Martha Longhurst and Minnie Caldwell and asked him why. He replied that he had a bit of a crush on Annie Walker, the landlady of the Rovers Return at that time but we were not to tell Lady Wendy or write about it. Now he's lost the ability to read anything more complicated than a drinks menu we think we're on safe ground with the doddery old duffer.

But poking fun at such a great man is not why we're here and, after all, Cranbourne Lanbourne meets that objective more than adequately. Now in his nineties Padraig had assumed the title of His Lordship and control of the dynasty in 1965 and had already married Wendy Geek Geek by that time. While local to Essex Wendy had met Padraig some years earlier while he was visiting Billericay to turn on the Christmas lights as the guest celebrity. Wendy recalls Padraig's generosity as he spent valuable time signing autographs for all seven people who turned up for the event. She commented at the time that it was a mistake to schedule the Christmas Carnival and the "switching on" of the Billericay Illuminations at the same time as an episode of Z Cars was showing on TV.

Lord Padraig inherited a substantial business and property empire. His position as Chairman of the Conisbrough Board (a modern tradition started by his grandfather in the 1870s when the Conisbrough dynasty members met three times a year to keep tabs on ongoing business ventures and projects and monitor progress in established areas) had seen him oversee dramatic change. Indeed it was the pace of change (compared with previous centuries when things moved at a gentle pace) that he regarded as the most remarkable and yet dangerous feature of the 20th century in commerce.

By way of an example Lord Padraig described the dynasty shareholdings in various railway, steel and coal mining companies all of which were purchased from the Conisbroughs in the 40s and 50s when the government embarked on a policy of nationalisation. Acting on advice from Cranbourne Lanbourne much of the dynasty fortune gleaned from these nationalised ventures was invested in TV, film studios and the manufacture of electrical goods – all of which seemed to be taking off in post-war Britain. His Lordship had merely followed his father's lead.

The relatively modest brewing concerns were retained together with some treacle mining, oil production in Lincolnshire and arable and livestock farming across the north and Midlands but the mills had all but disappeared. The world had changed shape and the dynasty had changed with it – often ahead of the game. One of His Lordship's deepest regrets was to lose so many loyal employees as the labour intensive industries slowly wound down and nothing substantive was put in place to replicate them. Conisbrough was proud that he and his associates in the Conservative government of the day did all they could at that time to relieve the misery.

Conisbrough, again acting on advice from Cranbourne Lanbourne, had entered the financial services industry and Padraig chaired a number of these family owned companies including Conisbrough Savings Bank. Lord Padraig resisted the temptation to manage dodgy European deposits from

Italy and the Eastern bloc much to Lanbourne's dismay and settled for obscure offshore and Channel Island client accounts put forward by Cranbourne as a safer alternative. It had ended in tears for the holding company which purchased the bank from the Conisbroughs some years back and the Chief Executive is still only halfway through his 40 year sentence for an unimaginable list of crimes associated with drugs, terrorism and money laundering transactions that, strangely, never made it on to Cranbourne Lanbourne's ledger when the Serious Fraud Office, MI5 and MI6 became involved.

So nowadays what remain beyond those industries mentioned above are Conisbroughphone Warehouse and the Amazbrough online retail empire – more than enough to keep Padraig and Wendy in the manner to which they've become accustomed – and an interesting legacy for the next generation when that time comes.

Dieter Teeters

While we're in the mood for "killing off" or, at least, "retiring" all the main characters it's time for an update from Cologne as it seems it's not only Lord Padraig who is suffering mental health frailties. For so long a pillar of his family, Dieter Dangelhosen has been hospitalised (or should it be imprisoned?) in a secure facility down the Grembergerring Strasse.

We're told Dieter came to the attention of the Polizei a couple of times before the state intervened and put him somewhere safe. The first occasion was at a "members only" gentleman's club in one of those narrow backstreets up behind the cathedral where he had attempted to gain entry claiming to be Lord Padraig Conisbrough. Complete with Padraig's business card (no reason why he shouldn't have been in possession of one) he had circumvented the first layer of security and had accessed the club proper. Events took a turn for the worse when Dieter ordered beer, sausage and the services of an identical twins double act using a credit account. Obviously distracted by the music, atmosphere and jangling of chains Dieter was unable to verify the PIN number.

When we contacted the Conisbroughs about their understanding of the incident which befell their cousin, with the suggestion that impersonation had taken place, Lord Padraig said that his memory wasn't what it was. When we offered a few reminders he spluttered something incomprehensible about "possibly being taken there once against my will by Lanbourne to meet some German business associates" down the telephone but you could hear Lady Wendy's eyebrows being raised from some distance. It remains shrouded in mystery.

Or at least it did until we were able to obtain the security CCTV from Golden Rain, the club concerned. Although there is no sound (a blessing in disguise perhaps) after several hours of painstaking research from numerous angles it is clear that the identical twins, Shackle and Tackle – doubtless unhappy at the loss of a customer – appeared to feed Dieter his beer and sausage without him even needing to ask. Unfortunately, as the Polizei arrived, the camera reveals that they had not placed the tasty wurst in Dieter's mouth and the officers were confronted with a man with his trousers down in a respectable club with large quantities of tomato ketchup and mild mustard near his rear end.

A police caution followed. Cranbourne Lanbourne, presumably not realising we would make the connection and even less that we would write about it, confirmed to us that they received an invoice from Golden Rain on Lord Conisbrough's account for food, drink, entry fees, sundries x 2 (we wonder!) and carpet cleaning that they would be disputing – if necessary meeting with the aggrieved parties at the club.

But there was worse to follow. Dieter had managed to wriggle out of one of the windows at his rooms at the

Dangelhosen's house in Cologne where he was being supervised by professionals appointed by the family. His nursing contingent reported that there was no outdoor clothing or appropriate shoes in his room and he couldn't have gone far given the freezing temperatures. In fact, walking a few hundred meters Dangelhosen ended up on Cologne South railway station with a long lens camera. The station abuts the university and it would seem Dangelhosen was taking candid images of the students in their rooms at the hall of residence and as they made their way along the platforms.

After receiving numerous complaints an officer arrived to interview Dieter who claimed to be a train spotter and was there in pursuit of his hobby. Unfortunately his flash card contained no images of the rich variety of passenger and freight operation but several hundred close ups of the students. He might still have got away with it had he not been wearing carpet slippers (everyone knows train spotters wear anoraks and sandals with socks), had his shirt not been slashed to the waist and been sporting a baseball cap with the message "Show the Old Fella' what you've got". He had also consumed several bottles of beer purchased at the market by the entrance to the platforms; judging by his trousers he had tried and failed to eat several salami baguettes.

Dangelhosen's son was summoned to the police station to collect Dieter who objected rather too strongly, not at the caution and final warning but confiscation of the flash card, and talked himself neatly in to further formal charges on public order grounds. Dieter's son was advised by the police doctor who examined the frail Dieter, that the family physicians should be alerted immediately as there appeared to be worrying trends developing based on the evidence of the two incidents.

The third (and, mercifully, final) incident took place at Cologne's main railway station while Dieter was out for a celebratory New Year dinner with the family and some friends at a nearby *Bierhaus*. Unfortunately for them Dieter had been cunning in showing some real signs of returning to normal aided by the cocktail of drugs administered by his 24 hour nursing contingent. Dangelhosen had been out on his own but supervised from a discreet distance by one of his nurses who declared him to be on the road to recovery. Of course devilish Dieter had not been swallowing all the pills he should have done – using a technique he had perfected over the years when obliged to drink French beer at business functions.

Escaping the party Hollywood movie-style by pretending to need the toilet and disappearing out of the back door it had been Dieter's maniacally conceived idea to emulate an English Lord he had heard of and disappear by taking the sleeper service train to Russia. Although he succeeded in purchasing a ticket Dieter, struggling badly to keep a lid on his perception of reality, had failed to recognise the need for a passport and visa. Losing control rapidly Dieter emerged into the night air outside the ticket office and was overcome by the noise, lights, the seething mass of people. He did the only thing that made any sense to him at that moment and dropped his trousers.

The mayhem that followed involving dozens of women just out minding their own business would have been a different kind of national embarrassment and would have destroyed the reputation and standing of his family had a Syrian asylum seeker not been arrested moments later further down the street performing in a similar manner to Dieter. The police or media, we have no idea which organisation, focused not on an outrage perpetrated by a prominent industrialist but some guy who wasn't used to alcohol and whose visa had expired. The Mayor and Chief of Police both resigned – we are told this was a consequence of their failure in office. We all know they were not prepared to play the silly game that had been initiated. Dieter would have read about it in his newspaper in the hospital had he not been holding it upside down.

One and Five Fifteen

We'd have dearly liked this story to end on a positive note but that's not how things turn out in real life. Unfortunately Lord Padraig Conisbrough had been spending increasing time at his home in Billericay due to his deteriorating mental health. Although his debility was nowhere near as severe as Dieter's the peace and quiet of Conisbrough Castle might have offered an alternative method of managing Lord Padraig's condition. Lady Geek Geek needed more than the sleepy northern backwater had to offer despite the luxury and facilities they enjoyed at the castle.

If truth be told, Lady Geek Geek had become a huge fan of Essex again; Wetherspoons' Blue Boar in Billericay and their trademark steak and kidney pudding and chips – not to mention the succulent range of Sauvignon Blanc wines – were proving irresistible diversions from His Lordship's deteriorating state of mind. While the Blue Boar had thrived alongside the dynasty in Billericay for generations Lady Conisbrough had been the first member of the family to take such a liking to the establishment.

Her Ladyship's other passion was games. We know she was an accomplished contract bridge player but she had, as the years rolled by, formed a liking bordering on addiction for bingo and the magnificent Mecca halls across Essex. At first this pursuit, which Lord Padraig had made clear he found filthy and disgusting had been kept secret from His Lordship but Higson had informed on Lady Wendy. Lady Geek Geek had, apparently, "borrowed" one of Higson's bottles of sherry and had failed to replace it causing the falling out.

Padraig was no longer in a position to question or understand Lady Geek Geek's not so well hidden passion and his doctors became increasingly concerned for him and referred His Lordship to specialists at Southend Victoria Hospital. The diagnosis was not encouraging for his consultant, Professor Pink an expert in atrophying brain tissue, declared he had a rare and thus far incurable disorder which was still being referred to by the world of medical professionals as "yellow 15". Lord Padraig Conisbrough was told he had weeks to live.

Understandably the revelation did little to cheer His Lordship's mood. His temper deteriorated further when Lady Geek Geek took him to bingo in Brentwood. With Higson enjoying a day off it fell to Her Ladyship to supervise her increasingly inconsistent and irrational husband. Padraig's nerves were eased slightly when advised that the bingo hall had a bar with waitress service. Settling down to his entertainment for the afternoon and evening Lord Conisbrough promptly won the Cashline for £1800. Fifteen minutes later he had won £2500 on Noel Edmunds' Deal or No Deal 80 ball game; then £4000 on the house 90 ball game. Not content with that Padraig added £27000 by taking the Essex-wide game and brought the house down by claiming the national monthly jackpot of £148000.

The manageress and most of her staff came up to Padraig to congratulate him and obtain publicity shots for the local newspapers and the Mecca organisation but couldn't understand Padraig's less than enthusiastic demeanour as he failed to smile for yet another photo opportunity. "I've got yellow 15", announced Padraig. "Heaven preserve us" replied the manageress "you've won the bloody raffle as well".

Glossary

Blackadder – an amusing fictional character created for TV

Boadicea – also known as Boudica she was a warrior and Queen of the Iceni (ancient Britons) who led a revolt against the Roman occupiers

Brian Rix – actor and active campaigner on behalf of those with learning difficulties. Particularly well known for his farces at the Whitehall Theatre and on TV

Chesterflood – imaginary Derbyshire town. Could be confused with Chesterfield which also has a church with a crooked spire

Great Conisbrough Railway – a fictitious company probably based loosely on the Great Central Railway

Hemel Sprot – a flanimal invented by Ricky Gervais for his book of the same name. Hemel and the place Sprotbrough, or sprots featuring here, have no connection to our knowledge

Kelham Island Pale Rider – a beer from a brewery in Sheffield that grew out of the Fat Cat pub in Alma Street. Any Kelham Island beer is worthy of special attention

Lord Somersby – star of the Somersby cider ads who nearly hijacked this story with their strap line of unreal histories

The M18 – modern road approximately 26 miles long built in 1967 and linking Goole and Rotherham (near Conisbrough)

Mecca Bingo – indescribable place of entertainment and gaming

Noel Edmunds Deal or No Deal – needs no introduction as a popular and entertaining television game show with many spin offs

Paul Daniels and Debbie McGee – a highly underrated contemporary magician and alleged entertainer and his wife/assistant. This novel was completed before the sad news of Paul's passing was received. RIP.

Specsavers – British based chain of opticians believed to have derived their name from Henny Hotbox

Starburst Mobile Catering – a fictitious company which has no connection with East Midlands Trains, operator of the services to Nottingham

Tanquaray – a brand of gin made by Charles Tanquaray Ltd – it's actually rather nice

Wetherspoons – national chain of purveyors of good quality food and drink at reasonable prices